THE LAND OF EIGHTEEN DREAMS

by

Lawrence J. Epstein

BookLocker.com, Inc.
2012

First Edition

Dedication

For Sharon, of course.

PROLOGUE

I have told my family and friends so many tales about my grandfather that they asked me to collect them. These are some episodes in my life, moments when a young and fragile self met my grandfather's guiding hand and wise words. I later learned that those words often echoed Jewish folk sayings.

I arranged the book chronologically so that my grandfather's story is told in order. As I read it over, I realized his tale was like that of many Eastern European Jews. He represented a whole people to me. My story in this book is not so chronological. Most of the stories are from my youth when I spent the most time with him. From my point of view, all these episodes are told in the same young voice and took place at the same time, long ago, and in the same place, the Land of Eighteen Dreams.

But that's to come. Let me start at the beginning, when my grandfather's sister saved him after he was kidnapped by the Russian army.

CHAPTER ONE:
LILY'S STORY

I was eight years old when I gave up on God. I didn't think I was speaking to anyone when I prayed. I didn't even understand why people thought there was a God. And I had figured out by then that I had a choice about whether or not to believe, and that I had a right to challenge what anyone else told me to think.

This little revolt of mine might have passed unnoticed except for the fact that my father was then president of our congregation. I'm not sure if my parents were more concerned about my father's reputation or the future destination of my soul, but they marched me directly into the rabbi's office. He was kind, and he smiled. But he provided me with no convincing proof of the Divine.

My parents were befuddled. Finally, after a series of family huddles, it was decided that I had a passing heresy, one that would disappear with maturity. My grandmother wasn't so sure. She called one day and told my mother that my grandfather wanted to tell me a story.

I loved my grandfather. He was gruff, but he loved my mother. I could see that. And so one Sunday grandma and grandpa came over. As if by some understanding, right after we ate the meal but before dessert everyone else left the dining room. My grandfather and I were alone.

He stretched his legs out and sighed. His eyes closed and, though seated, he seemed to rock his body back and forth. I don't know even now if he was praying or remembering or what. Finally, he was done.

Then he looked at me and said, "So I heard my little granddaughter is not on such good terms with God."

"We don't speak," I said.

He scratched his head. "More's the pity for God. You have a lot to say. You know when I was just your age I didn't believe in God either. But then something happened. Can I tell you about it?"

"What was it?"

"My sister Lily saved me after I was kidnapped by the Russian army."

"How did she do it?"

"Ah, that's the story. Do you want to hear it?"

I nodded. "Tell me, from the beginning." I always liked stories. I wondered how my grandfather knew that.

"Good," he said. "I must start by telling you about our town in Russia. It was terrible there for little boys when they turned eight. Our town had to have a quota of young boys who would go into the army of the Czar, the man who ruled Russia. My cousin Mendel, he was seven then but big, and they didn't have the quota, so the town's leaders changed the birth record and sent poor Mendel off with the Russian militia who came for the boys. Some boys cut off a finger, and even with that, the army might take them."

"What happened to the boys?"

"It was very bad for them. They went to camps. In our town they were sent to Siberia first for ten years. And then at 18 they served in the Czar's army for 25 years. The Russians would feed bacon and ham to the yeshiva boys. No one could learn at all about being Jewish. They couldn't pray. They weren't near any Jewish women.

"That's what happened to Mendel. He was gone. We didn't talk about him too much. We were scared to mention his name in front of his mother because when we did she ran into her house and cried. His story always frightened the rest of us. When we heard about him many years later he had married some Russian woman whose father had some business contacts with Mendel's commander."

Then my grandfather paused to control his anger. "And in the whole town where we lived, do you know who was the worst of the lot?"

I shook my head.

His voice rose, letting loose that anger inside. "It was Anshel, the butcher's brother. May his name be cursed. This Anshel was a chapper. That means he hunted little Jewish boys for the Czar. He got money for all those he turned over to the army. May he burn in Gehenna for a thousand generations."

I didn't know what Gehenna was, but it didn't sound good.

"And it was Anshel"--he paused and made a spitting sound—"who captured me, my little rose." My grandfather always called me his little rose when I was a small child. He loved flowers and gave them often to my grandmother.

"Anshel and the soldiers. They hid in some trees right by the field where I played in the afternoon after school. I was running around with the other boys, and then I went on my way toward home because it was getting dark. Suddenly, he jumped out from behind and grabbed me. I was so little, I didn't have a chance. I tried to kick and scream, but the soldiers had me by then. The other boys saw them but they could not help. They ran for their lives.

"The soldiers took me to a camp near the town. I was to stay there for three months before going off to Siberia. They gave me a uniform and shoes that were way too big. And bad food. I cried each day. I thought I was lost. But I hadn't counted on Lily."

"Was she older than you, grandpa?"

He nodded. "She was twelve. And a beauty. And the bravest person in the whole world, my little rose. And wise. She would hear one word and understand two."

9

"What did she do to help you?"

"What did she do? Ah, she was Deborah and David and Esther and Samson. She was Robin Hood and Zorro and the Lone Ranger. And all in the same person.

"So I was late coming home from playing. My mama and papa and Lily were frantic. I was a good boy, and I was never late. There were chores to do at home. They feared the worst. They searched and searched and finally found a friend of mine. He told them what had happened. They went home and cried.

"My parents and Lily went to the rabbi. He said he could not help, that no one could. He said I was gone, that it was the lot of the Jews, that God would protect me, but that I could not be saved. The rabbi didn't know me too well because I would sneak out of shul to play. And maybe I didn't always go to cheder.

"I was like you, my little rose. I thought this God was not so good an idea. Anyway, the rabbi didn't help. No one helped. They all told my parents and my sister to forget about me.

"And they tried to do so. Of course they couldn't. But they came to believe that they could not save me. Everyone believed that."

"But not your sister Lily."

"No, my dear, not Lily. She would not give up.

"I had been in the camp for a few weeks. But even from the first day Lily had a plan. The day after I was gone, she went to the tavern in our town. She said she would cook and clean and sweep in return for the big wine barrels when they were empty. My Lily had gone to work at age six as a servant for other families taking care of little children, so she knew how to work. I don't know where she found the time, but she worked in that tavern whenever she could. Remember, she had a lot to do at home and at her job as a servant girl. Slowly, over those weeks while I was in the camp, she collected the empty barrels.

"Finally, she had enough. When she was ready, she got a big basket. And a blanket. Then she made strudel with lots of fruit in it. This recipe she learned from our mother, whose own mother had come from Austria and made strudel there. Then Lily packed two bottles of vodka she had borrowed from the tavern where she worked."

"You don't really mean borrowed, do you grandpa?"

"It's better to say borrowed."

"Okay, grandpa."

"So, she had this big basket with the strudel and bottles of vodka and the blanket and what she had hidden under the blanket. Then she sneaked outside and went to get our horse and wagon. She drove the wagon to where she had hidden the empty wine barrels, and even though they were heavy and awkward she picked them up and piled them in the wagon, just as she had practiced.

"It was still very early in the day when she started out, a little girl driving that wagon and heading for the camp to try to rescue me. What must have been going through her head. What fear she must have felt, but what steel underneath.

"She decided that before she left the town she would first stop off to pray. She went to a field where there were many brightly-colored flowers. She told me she just stood there and begged the Almighty for strength and guidance. Now, the Almighty was probably like the rabbi and didn't know me very well I would guess. Maybe she had to tell the Almighty who I was. Anyway, when she was finished she got back in the cart and faced the horse in the direction of the camp.

"It was almost noon when she got there. She stopped out of sight of the camp to make sure the barrels were still in place. And then she drove up to the guard post and smiled at the Russian standing there. Now, remember, Lily was very pretty, like you are. She said hello. She handed one of the bottles of vodka to the Russian. Believe me, you can bet he liked that. Then she said her brother was in the camp and it was my birthday, so she wanted to bring me some strudel. She gave him a piece. He liked it. He asked about the wine barrels, and she said they were empty and she was supposed to be bringing them to winemaker to fill them for her father who owned a tavern."

"She lied, grandpa?"

"She told a truth that was higher than the regular truth."

"Oh."

"The guard wasn't sure what to do. He checked to make sure the wine barrels were really empty. He wanted the wine, you see. Finally he agreed she could go in as long as she stayed no longer than fifteen minutes.

"She drove the wagon as fast as she dared, yelling out my name, asking the other boys where I was. Someone came in to tell me there was a screaming girl with a horse and wagon calling out my name and looking for me. I ran outside following her voice, and then I saw her. Lily and I hugged each other tightly. We were both crying.

"She told me to go inside quickly. We were alone in the barracks then. Suddenly from the bottom of her basket underneath the blanket she pulled out my clothes and shoes. She had cleaned the clothes. I asked her what I was to do. She told me I had to change into my clothes. Then, when I was ready, she would go outside. I would wait for a minute while she took off the top of one of the barrels and then began to turn the wagon around. When the back of the wagon faced the door, I was supposed to run outside and hide in the open barrel.

"I told her such a trick wouldn't work, that I wouldn't fit. She refused to listen to me. She said I was to trust her. That she had measured the barrel. That she knew I would escape. Then she turned her back, and I got out of my uniform and put on my own clothes. The shoes made my feet feel much better.

"She went outside first and got into the wagon. I peeked out. When the wagon had turned I dashed outside and immediately saw the open barrel. I crawled into it. There was just enough room. She jumped off the wagon and put the top on the barrel. I could hardly move or breathe, and I was very scared.

"Lily began driving the wagon out. The guard stopped her, but she handed him the second bottle of vodka and the remaining strudel. He took them and put them down. Then he walked slowly around the whole wagon. I couldn't see, but I knew we were stopped for a long time. He opened one of the barrels. He must have been too lazy to check them all because he didn't open mine. Finally he let her through.

"My sister Lily drove a half mile. Then she took off the top so I could breathe and drove us the rest of the way home. I don't think my mama and papa stopped crying for three whole days. And that's how Lily saved me from the Czar."

"Is that what made you believe in God, grandpa?"

"Yes. At least in my own way. After that, I believed in kindness and bravery and good deeds. And I thought whenever I saw those, why that's what everyone else called God. Without Lily I would not have escaped. And you, my little rose, you would not ever have been born. Or your mother either."

That stopped me. I looked at him. "Do you pray to God, grandpa?"

"I pray to God to give me strength and guidance so I can help people and help myself. And I cheat a little. I ask God to protect you and everyone else in the family, and all the good and innocent people in the world."

"Do you think God listens?"

"I don't know, but I do think God gave strength to Lily when she prayed in that field of flowers. That's why I believe."

I paused for a minute. "And after that? What happened after she saved you, grandpa?"

"Oh, right after she saved me and before the army could come looking for me my family decided it was time to go to the Golden Land. So we took our wagon and we left very fast. They smuggled me out again, this time hiding under some hay they took from a nearby farmer who didn't like Jews."

"You mean they borrowed the hay."

"Yes, yes. I mean they borrowed.

"And let me tell you it was not so easy to get to Hamburg where we got the boat to America. Lots of gonifs along the way who wanted our money, I can tell you that. But we got here."

"Tell me what happened to everyone when you got to America, grandpa."

"Ah, my little rose, the tides go in and they go out. Life shifts all the time. My poor papa could not make a living here. He tried all he could. But he was honest in his business dealings. A very bad trait according to some people. He grew sick and died. And my mama, she lived for some years after him. But it was really only her body that lived on. She truly died the same day he did. Only she kept walking. It was very sad to see. Very hard for all of us.

"But I loved this country. I worked hard. I found your grandma one day and we got married."

"Grandma says she's not sure how she puts up with you."

"Endless patience, I think. But she made three wonderful children. And then they made children. And that's where you come in."

I smiled. Then I asked what happened to the people in the old country, the ones who stayed.

My grandfather shook his head. "Very sad. Mostly they were killed in the whirlwind, by the man with the little moustache in Germany or the man with the big moustache in Russia. I dare not say their names. But what happened to Mendel's family is another story."

"I thought you said he married a Russian woman."

"He did indeed. And they had children. And their children had children. And it was in those grandchildren that the pintele yid burned."

"What's that, grandpa?"

"The pintele yid? Why it's the holy spark in every Jewish soul. It can't go out. Sometimes it does not burn too brightly, but it is always there, always ready to come to life. Right now it's burning low in you, my little rose, but it's there. In Mendel's grandchildren the pintele yid shined brightly."

"What did they do, grandpa?"

"Mendel's grandchildren somehow found out my address in America and wrote to me. They wrote and said one day they or their children would be free to leave. They wanted to go to Israel, to live in Jerusalem. Maybe one day the Soviets will let the Jews out. And then Mendel's descendants will live in the Jewish homeland. Maybe one day when you grow older you'll get to see them."

"Can I see their pintele yid?"

My grandfather laughed. "No, my little rose, you can't see it. But you can feel it inside yourself. Lily felt it."

"How come I never met Lily?"

He sighed and sat still for a while, looking at the wall toward the painting of the bridge over a stream next to a wooden cottage. When he spoke his voice was very low. "Lily died, my little one. She went painting one day in the woods in Maine and drank from the river. Then she got sick and died."

"Is that why mama named me Lily?"

"Yes, it is. You've got the best name in the world. And one day you'll grow up to be brave and good like my sister. And I hope you'll tell her story to your grandchildren."

"I will tell her story, grandpa."

"I know you will. And I could tell you other stories about her, and not just in the old country. On the boat over, and living here,"

"Tell me some, grandpa."

And my grandfather would picture his sister and smile.

"All right. But first let's have some of that strudel your grandma has made for dessert."

CHAPTER TWO:
THE ESCAPE

"I hate him, grandpa."

"He's your brother, Lily."

"I don't care. He always gets whatever he wants."

"Still, you shouldn't have done it."

I sat quietly, trying to look as sullen as I could.

"I'm glad I did it, grandpa."

"And you're glad you're in this room with no television? Glad your mama won't let any friends come over after school? Glad you can't call anyone?"

"She'd never do that to Will. He's an angel in mama's eyes. It's not fair."

"You have to apologize to your brother, Lily."

"No, grandpa. I won't do it."

"I can see you're sorry."

"I'm not sorry."

"Yes you are. The face is the worst informer. I can see your face. Your mama said you have to be punished until you apologize."

"Then I'll be punished for the rest of my life."

"Do you think what you did was right, Lily? What would you have said if Will did it to you?"

"He wouldn't do it. He's an angel."

"You didn't answer my question. Was what you did, right?"

I paused.

"Maybe not."

"When your brother's girlfriend calls him and you get the message, you have to tell him. That missed message caused great confusion. His girlfriend didn't understand why he didn't call back. They missed going someplace. Will goes off to college next year, and you'll miss him."

17

"I will not."

"You will. You'll see. I know it's hard to have a brother who's older than you are."

"He's seven years older, grandpa."

My grandfather pulled over a chair and sat down next to me.

"I was an older brother, and I wasn't always such a good brother."

"You, grandpa?"

"Come. Your mama will let you take a walk with me. We'll go to the bench behind the building."

We lived in Jackson Heights, in Queens, in an apartment complex called Garden Bay Manor. The buildings were two stories, attached to each other, made to appear as though they were built with Tudor brick. In my building, there was a basement and a family upstairs. The girl who lived there was about my brother's age and played a lot of music. Once she had a party in the basement, and I had to cover my ears to fall asleep.

The area behind my building was open. It had trees and unfilled land and a few benches. All the children in the neighborhood used it and others like it as play areas. There wasn't a back door to the apartments, so we had to walk to the end of the block to reach the back yard area.

When my grandfather and I were finally seated, he said.

"I lied at Yussel's funeral."

I looked over at my grandfather.

His brother, the one he called Yussel and everyone else called Jack, had died recently, and my whole family had attended the funeral.

"What do you mean, grandpa?"

"I didn't always love my brother because I thought he was a schlemiel. I mean who gets buried right after Rosh Hashanah and on the very day that the Dodgers finally win the World

THE LAND OF EIGHTEEN DREAMS

Series? Who misses Johnny Podres throw a game like that? A schlemiel, that's who."

"Were you angry at him, grandpa?"

He looked at me. "Sometimes when I think of him, I get angry. But more than at him, I'm angry at the world because I'll miss him so much and because the world was so hard for Yussel. It was the world that made him a schlemiel. The world is a tough place for the living."

"You made a nice speech, grandpa. I heard everyone tell you that."

"I did my best."

"Then why did you say you lied?"

My grandfather stretched his legs. "Everyone invents a bit of the truth at a funeral, like the person only did good. And that part was true. Yussel only did do good. But I didn't tell the whole truth about him."

"Then why did you lie, grandpa?"

"I lied for your mama and your aunts and all the families and for Yussel's son. And maybe I lied for me, too. Maybe I was too scared to tell the truth."

"The truth about what, grandpa?"

"What are you, a lawyer?"

"Sorry, grandpa."

He sighed. "No, I'm sorry, my little one. Sometimes you have to ignore the way my words come out. They can be loud like thunder, but I don't mean them. Especially to you. I'm upset with me, not you."

"You can talk to me about Yussel, grandpa. I'm nine years old now. I won't tell anyone, not even mama."

"I know you won't. Yussel's story is part of when we left Russia. That was right after my sister saved me. It's fifty-seven years. And it's in front of my eyes like it happened an hour ago."

"You'll feel better if you tell me, grandpa."

He laughed.

"And I want to hear how you got out of Russia. I remember about the hay."

"I can still smell it. " He paused for a few seconds. "So, you want to hear, do you? Maybe I should tell it, just so I can remember Yussel once again. I miss him every day.

"First of all, my mama didn't want to go. She thought she could hide me with a cousin in another town."

"I thought everyone wanted to come to America, grandpa."

He shook his head. "The young, but not the religious people, not so many old people. Most of them stayed. They made a very bad choice, but nobody knew it then. They all should have left.

"My mama had been born there. Her friends were there. She…"

"She what, grandpa?"

"In a few more years I will tell you."

"I know a little girl who had a grandpa who said he would teach her to play the violin. And then he died, and she never learned."

"You're not making me feel so good."

"Sorry, grandpa."

"You think it's better I should tell you all now? In case I join Yussel?"

"I just want to know the story."

My grandfather closed his eyes and sat still. Finally, he looked at me and said, "My mama lost a baby. That was after me. Then she tried to have another baby, and that baby was born but died in two days." He paused. "This is not so nice to hear, Lily. Are you sure you want to hear it?"

"Yes, grandpa."

He gave a short nod. "My mama held the dead baby for a day and a half. She refused to believe it had died. She sang lullabies to it. My poor papa was going crazy. Finally, my mama accepted the truth. Then she gave papa the baby to bury and she lay down in her bed and didn't get up. She cried. My sister and I brought her soup. She wouldn't eat at first. Even when she did, it took many days before mama got up from the bed and stayed up. And then she couldn't have any more babies.

"So when papa said he wanted to leave, she kept screaming, 'First God gives me no more children, and now no more home.' She scared me. I didn't like to see my mama so upset. My papa kept telling her they would begin again. That America was new. And she said whatever she did her friends wouldn't be there to see it. She said that America was okay for the young, and the criminals, and the revolutionaries, but she wanted her friends to see her life, to be part of it."

"But she went, finally."

"Yes she did, my little one. Because of Lily. One night Lily spoke to her quietly. I listened when I should have been asleep. Lily told her that her family would be her witnesses, that papa needed a new chance, that I needed a life, that America was the land where the poor could get rich, where the Jews could walk in the streets with their heads up. That it was different because it was a whole land of immigrants. And after that night mama said she would go.

"We started out on a cold morning. We didn't take much. My mama took a big blanket and we took our pillows. Mama wouldn't give up her goosefeather pillow. And my papa, he took his prayer book and a mezuzah to put up on the doorpost of our next home. Lily cried because she had to leave almost all her books. She hadn't complained to mama about that. She just gave them to some children and she cried.

"And we brought food, all the food we could. I was the only one who didn't feel like I was leaving anything behind."

"Was Yussel with you then?"

"No, my little rose. It was mama, and papa, and Lily, and me. Papa drove the wagon fast. We were supposed to get passports and other papers but that took months and sometimes people would get passports and still couldn't leave. So we didn't get them. Papa brought some money to pay the smugglers to get us across the Russian border into Austria. From there we would be all right. We knew from others who had made the trip that we could get to Hamburg and get on a big ship to America."

"But Yussel told me that he was born in the Old Country, grandpa. Where was he born?"

"Ah, that story is coming right now, my little one."

"We had been riding all day. We were tired. It was getting dark. This was the time that my papa said the ghosts came out. Suddenly up ahead of us we heard crying and screaming on the side of the road. We listened. And there, almost hidden in the trees, there was a young woman. She was sobbing loudly. We couldn't very well just drive by her. We had to stop."

"Because she was crying?"

"Because she was in trouble. Everybody drives by the Jews whenever we are in trouble. We couldn't do that.

"When we got to her, I could see blood coming down the side of her head. It wasn't dried, but still red. And, there, next to her, was a small pistol."

"Someone shot her, grandpa?"

"No, Lily. She shot herself."

"But she wasn't dead."

"No, she was still alive."

She told us she was a Russian girl, not Jewish. She would not tell us her name or the name of her mama and papa."

"What was she doing on the road?"

"She had run away from home. Mama told me she looked about seventeen, only five years older than Lily. Very bloated face. She didn't have shoes. She..."

"She what, grandpa?"

"You can't tell anyone, Lily. Ever. Not until I'm gone. Not until your grandma is gone."

"But what if someone asks me? I can't lie, can I, grandpa?"

"Okay, if someone walks up to you and says, 'Now, Lily, you have to tell me the big secret about Yussel,' why then you can tell the story. But only then. And you can't cheat. You can't go around saying, 'Guess what I know about Yussel that no one else knows.'"

"I won't tell ever unless someone asks, grandpa."

"You hold onto the truth like it was your own mama, don't you, my little rose?"

"I guess so, grandpa."

"Okay, then. I trust you.

"The young woman we saw on the road was dying from the wound in her head. She told us that she had run away from home because her parents didn't want her any more. They were peasants, and she had been friends with a young man who was a revolutionary. They didn't like that, but then one day she told them she was going to have a baby. She was crying. She said the man she loved had been arrested by the soldiers and shot. She kept crying.

"She said she had gotten a ride from a man after she paid him. After riding for a while she asked him to stop. She got out because she felt dizzy. She walked over to some trees to lean against them. She could no longer see the wagon, but she heard it leaving. The man had taken off without her and left the poor girl alone. It was then, in despair, that she had shot herself.

"My mama told the girl that we would take care of her as we best could. Lily and my mama had both delivered babies, so that didn't scare them so much, but it scared me. The woman begged us for some food. We needed what we had, but we gave her food and water anyway. We stayed under the clump of trees that night. The stars blinked on and off all through the night like some big signal. I was very cold.

"I think it was about three in the morning. I had fallen asleep. Suddenly I heard the woman screaming. Lily had spread the blanket out on the ground. She didn't have what she needed, not even hot water. Lily held the woman's hand while my mama helped her give birth.

"Then I heard the baby crying, but I didn't hear the woman. My mama held the baby, and rocked it. My papa came over to me and sat down. He looked very serious. Then he told me the Russian woman had died. I asked him what would happen to the baby.

"'Your mama says we can't leave the baby, Benjamin,' he said to me. 'If we did he would die.'"

"And so, my little rose, we didn't leave the baby. But Jews couldn't be carrying around a Russian baby. God alone knows what they would say we wanted to do to the child. They might say we had kidnapped the little baby to drain its blood or some such nonsense the people talked about. And we couldn't return the baby to the grandparents because we didn't know them. And the baby's mama and papa were both dead."

"So you kept the baby? That was Yussel, grandpa?"

"That baby was Yussel. We pretended he was my brother and Lily's. I mean he was a baby. Nobody could say he didn't look like us."

"But he wasn't Jewish."

"Not exactly according to the Law, no. I can't say he was. We never told anyone until we got to Hamburg. We found a rabbi there and told him the whole story. Then the rabbi said the right blessings, and did some other things, and then Yussel the Russian became Yussel the Jew. "

"And your mama had a new baby."

"Yes she did, my little rose, a new baby to love. I think Yussel saved mama. All by himself."

"Then maybe he wasn't a schlemiel."

"Maybe he wasn't at that."

"Was Yussel surprised when you told him?"

"A bit. When he grew a little, he didn't look like us at all, but mama said he looked like her father and no one asked any questions, at least not in front of Yussel. He was surprised, that's for sure. But he decided not to tell anyone. That's how it became a secret. But Yussel was always a good Jew. He said he had to work extra hard at being a Jew because he wasn't born one."

"So he was born in the Old Country."

"Yes, barely. Because we were in a rush to get out.

"We had to stop in a big town to get what we needed for little Yussel. We had been avoiding the towns like that. But he needed to eat, so we got him what was called dried-milk food. We got a lot of that and a blanket to wrap him in and whatever else my mama could find. And then we were off again.

"Finally we got to the border. The town of Brody was right across the border. From there we could get help going to Berlin by train in a special car for immigrants and then to Hamburg.

"My papa waited until it was dark and then drove to the house we had to go to. Papa and I went inside, and everyone else waited in the wagon. The men in the house scared me. The older one, the father, had a face that had a lot of marks on it. Like scars or a skin disease. He spoke to papa, and told him how much it would cost. Papa paid him the money, and the man and his two sons came outside and told us to leave the wagon.

We had no choice. Everyone carried a small bundle, and we started walking.

"We crossed a meadow, and the father stopped often, listening for sounds. When we got very near the border and could see where the guards stayed, the father said we had to wait for the guards to chase other smugglers. Then the way would be clear.

"After an hour, this man with the scary face said he had to search Lily because he thought he saw her carrying a weapon."

"He just wanted to touch her, right grandpa?"

"Right."

"What did she do?"

"Why she looked him in the eye, and said, 'Go ahead. But don't blame me if you get cholera, because I've got it.' At the time, everyone was scared of cholera, scared they'd get it and die. The man didn't know if she was lying, but it was dark and he couldn't really see her too well. He finally decided not to take a chance."

"Lily was brave."

"That she was. And fast. I mean just as soon as he asked, she was ready. If she had hesitated, he would have thought she was making it up. But he didn't want to take a chance, so he stayed away from her.

"Another half-hour passed, and the ugly man went up to my papa. He said, it was taking longer than he thought and papa had to pay him more money. But my papa said he didn't have any more, and the man said he was going home, and we could cross the border on our own.

"Then Lily walked up to papa and said, 'Oh, papa, don't you remember you gave me this little bit of extra money for these men?' And she handed him some more."

"Where did the money come from?"

"Lily had carried it from home. It was money she had saved from her work as a servant girl. All those little children she had helped. But we needed it now.

"Papa wasn't happy. He knew these men were thieves, but he gave over the money. And right after that we heard the guards running. Then we began walking again. Soon we stopped, and the man told us we were in Austria."

"Then what happened, grandpa?"

"So much I can't remember it all. It happened so fast. But I can still see the red building in Hamburg and the dirty cots lined up along the wall. They gave us boiled potatoes and sliced white bread for breakfast."

He stopped and looked at me."But you didn't ask me the question I thought you would, my little rose."

"What's that, grandpa?"

"I thought you would ask if little Yussel cried as we waited because if he cried the border guards might have found us."

"Why didn't he cry?"

"Because my mama held him close and sang a lullaby in his ear and fed him. She really loved Yussel. And we were happy about that."

"I didn't know Yussel so well. But he was very nice to me. He taught me how to draw faces."

"I know, my little one. My sister Lily taught him. He was an artist. Not good enough to make a living. There was so much he was not good enough at to make a living. Every business went into it was like there was a curse on him. He had a pushcart and he'd come home with no money and more goods because he bought from other carts. He tried to make clothing and suddenly it seemed people didn't need new trousers. Maybe this was because Yussel didn't believe in using a tape measure, so his trousers didn't always go down as far as they should on one customer or maybe they went too far on another. So many jobs and never any money. And he married when he was very old."

"I never saw his wife, grandpa."

"I know. She died when she gave birth to little David."

"I like David."

My grandfather nodded. "A very nice boy. It's very sad for him. But we will all help. I said he could live with grandma and me for a short while. There is another cousin in Brooklyn who will take him into her home."

"But you're old, grandpa."

"So David should live on the streets? Anyway, better old than dead. He'll be all right. It's just for a short while. He's a nice boy."

My grandfather sighed. "A tough life for Yussel. Always looking for luck and never finding it. But kind to everyone else. He was never jealous. He always helped others even if they did what he wanted to do but couldn't."

"Did people feel sorry for him, grandpa?"

"A little. But everyone loved him. He gave to those with even less than he had. He was kind to everyone, especially the sick. He would go to the Jewish homes where the old people lived. He sang for them. Yussel always had a nice voice, and he remembered the songs my mama taught him. And he would go visit the sick when no one else would go, the people who scared everyone, even people in their own family, because the Angel of Death was standing by their beds. But Yussel stayed right beside them even as their flesh was falling off, even...oh, I'm sorry, my little rose. I didn't mean to upset you."

"I'm not upset, grandpa. You once told me I had to be tough or the world would beat me."

"So I did."

"What else did Yussel do for the sick?"

"He brought them soup. He sat and talked with them, about the old days, about the World to Come if they wanted, about the Dodgers, and, now this was only for the dying, he would even find some kind words to say about the Yankees. And he…"

I waited for a minute, but my grandfather was silent. "What are you thinking, grandpa?"

"I'm sorry, my little one. I was just remembering some words my papa used to say when he was old. He spoke in Yiddish, of course, but his words meant that sometimes it is only in loss that one heart understands another."

"What does that mean, grandpa?"

"It means that I have been the schlemiel. Now, and only now, I understand that Yussel was a rich man indeed. So rich in goodness that maybe he was a Lamedvavnik."

"What's that grandpa?"

"A Lamedvavnik? That's one of only 36 people on Earth. We don't know who they are, and they don't know each other. But they are so good that they prove to God that it was right to create humans."

"I think you're a Lamedvavnik, grandpa."

"You're sweet to say so, Lily, but your grandpa is not one. As for Yussel, who knows? Maybe he was one."

He stood up. "Enough of my stories. Come, your mama will think we ran away with the circus."

I reached out to hold my grandfather's hand, and we walked back inside.

It was just as we reached my apartment that my grandfather turned to me and said, "It would have been better if I appreciated Yussel more in his life, if I understood him from the inside. Do you understand what I'm saying?"

"You're saying I should understand Will."

My grandfather was silent.

I went back inside. Will was seated at the table. I sat down next to him and apologized. I said I hadn't meant to hurt him. I told him I would call his girlfriend and apologize to her. And I did.

Will did leave for college a year later. In a way he was too much older than I to have a close relationship, but when he left I cried for the relationship we might have had but didn't.

My brother and I got very close after I grew up. Sometimes at family gatherings we would tell the story of my grandfather's escape and about the day Will and I truly became brother and sister.

CHAPTER THREE:
DAN, THE ICE CREAM MAN

"Grandpa! Grandpa! I need some money. The ice cream man is here!"

He reached into his pocket without hesitation and gave me a dollar.

I liked to ask my grandfather for money because he always gave me extra. We had a ritual. I would offer him the change, and he would tell me to keep it to buy a book. I probably could have bought enough books to fill the Queensborough Public Library with all that change.

I loved the ice cream, of course, but what made it really special was buying it from Dan, the Ice Cream Man. He was an old man, tall and thin, with a dark, tanned face criss-crossed with lines. He spent the hot summer days pedaling around with a freezer of ice cream in front of him.

Dan believed in quizzes. Really, he believed in children. He'd give quizzes to all the children in the neighborhood, and if we got the question right he gave us free ice cream.

I was scared to ask him for a quiz. I was afraid of giving the wrong answer. Not only would I be deprived of ice cream, but I would also feel dumb. I used to lie in bed at night and imagine what quizzes Dan would give me. In my reverie, I always gave a brilliant answer. One night I decided my answer was so good that Dan would give me two ice cream cups.

I didn't want to ask anyone for help. After all, I was nine years old and thought I should be brave enough to ask Dan myself to give me a quiz.

It happened one day when I didn't expect it. A group of us were playing when my friend Barbara yelled out that Dan, the Ice Cream Man was coming. Barbara screamed for him, and he stopped. She turned to me.

"Okay, Lily. Today is the day. Today you have to ask Dan."

I was trapped. I felt a small amount of panic, but I held my fists tightly together. I couldn't face my friends as a continuing failure. I sighed and asked Dan for a quiz.

He took off his hat, looked down at me, and said, "So you want a quiz? All right. I've got one ready. How much is eight and six?"

I was fast with numbers then, and I knew the answer immediately. Indeed, the quiz was far simpler than others I'd heard him give. Still, not wanting to mess up my first quiz, I pondered the answer slowly. Had the rules arithmetic changed overnight, I wondered, or was the answer the same as it always was? No, the longer I stood there, the more I was sure that this was no trick. Dan didn't try to trick anyone. Finally, I smiled and said, "Fourteen."

"Very good. What kind of ice cream would you like, Lily?"

"A chocolate bar. And how did you know my name?"

"I'm friends with your grandfather. I've watched you grow up, running around the streets and playing games."

He handed me the ice cream.

"How do you know my grandpa?"

"Your grandfather is my oldest friend in America. Why his sister practically saved my sister's life."

"How did she?"

"I can't tell you now, Lily. I have to sell ice cream."

"Oh."

"Ask your grandfather. He'll tell you. And say hello for me."

My friends congratulated me as Dan pulled away. We said good-bye. I began to eat the ice cream as I walked back into the apartment. We lived on 80th Street. Grandpa didn't live in our apartment. There wasn't enough room, so he and grandma had recently moved into the apartment two doors down from us. He sometimes sat outside, looking up at the weeping willow tree in front of the buildings, but he was in my apartment very often. He spent much of his day reading. I never saw anyone read so many newspapers and books.

I came in holding the ice cream.

"It looks good," he said.

I nodded. "Dan, the Ice Cream Man says hello."

"A very good man. And it looks like he has very good ice cream."

I nodded. "Grandpa, he said he knew you. That your sister Lily saved his sister's life."

"In a way, I suppose she did."

"He said you would tell me the story."

"All right. But first let me make some tea while you finish that ice cream. He got up and made his way to the kitchen. Soon he sat down with his tea and began.

"It was on the boat, the boat coming to America. I've known Dan since then. A long time. We came over on a ship called the *Bulgaria*. All the immigrants remember the names of the ships they came on. The *Bulgaria* was big. It had four decks. During the day, when the sea was calm, we went up on deck. It was loud up there. Children were screaming and babies were crying. People played their music. Other people clapped their hands. And there was not much room. If we were lucky we found a chair on the deck. I can still see the two big masts. They told us there were more than 2,500 people on the ship, and almost all of them were in steerage."

"What's that, grandpa?"

"That was below the decks. A long time before I was on it the ship was steered from down there, so they still called it steerage. Let me tell you it was some place. They never cleaned in steerage. It smelled, well imagine the worst smell you can and this was worse. And so many people at night. There were cots all over the place, in stacks of three. We slept in our clothes. The man next to me was big. He would snore like Gabriel's horn. May his tonsils be cursed. And he was so close his shoulder touched mine until I moved. But if I turned around, the man on the other side had his face right next to me. And the boat rocked back and forth. Everyone got sick from the rocking. One man kept falling off his cot every time the boat moved.

"Mama and Lily and the baby were on the women's side. I don't think it was so good there, either, because some of the crew would come right in without knocking. They scared the girls so much some of them wouldn't even leave steerage after dark.

"How did you meet Dan?"

"Daniel he was called then, and he was a strange boy. All of the other boys and I played on deck, mostly marbles or dominoes. Daniel would stand off to the side. He never talked to anyone or ever played with us. He was traveling just with his sister, Reisel, so maybe he missed his mama and papa."

"If he didn't talk, how did you meet him grandpa?"

"You know boys get into fights. So a group of boys surrounded Daniel and they started yelling at him calling him bad names. And then one pushed him. And then they all started to push him."

"Did he fight back?"

"No. He should have, but he didn't."

"Why?"

"I don't know. He just stood there for some reason. Daniel didn't trust people, didn't think anyone was on his side. He had learned that everyone has enemies, but he hadn't learned that besides enemies everyone has friends."

"What happened to Daniel?"

"I may have punched the boy who was leading the others."

"You hit him, grandpa?"

"It's possible. And maybe I hit a few other boys, too. Who knows? Maybe after I hit some, the rest ran away."

"Mama told me not to hit anyone."

"That's good advice, my little one. Sometimes."

"You mean sometimes I should hit people?"

"Not to hurt them, just to protect yourself."

"My teacher says not to hit anyone either."

"Maybe your mama and your teacher didn't grow up in Russia. Maybe they haven't seen enough bad in the world."

I considered that. "Why did you save Daniel, grandpa?"

"Because he could not save himself. And because I could do it. Who helps the weak and sick, my little one, if not those strong enough to do so?"

"Is that when Daniel became your friend?"

"Sort of. He talked to me a bit, but he still didn't trust me, not until his sister's necklace was stolen."

"Who stole it?"

"His sister wasn't sure. She said she had an expensive gold necklace that she kept hidden behind the cots. There was a crewman we nicknamed Smokes because he often smoked a pipe. Daniel's sister thought she saw Smokes sneaking around, but she wasn't certain. Daniel told me his sister cried and cried, because the necklace had belonged to her mama, and it was her good luck charm, and her mama told her it was for an emergency in America. She could sell it if she needed. I told my sister, Lily, and she went to speak to Reisel. When she was done, Lily said Daniel and I should search the crew area where Smokes stayed to see if we could find the necklace.

"So that afternoon, Lily went over to talk with Smokes."

"She pretended to like him?"

"A bit. Just to keep him talking for a while so he wouldn't catch us.

"Daniel and I went to where the crew stayed. We waited until no one was around and we went into the area. I was very scared we would get caught and I would get sent back to Russia without my mama and papa. But Lily told me to do it, and I trusted her and because she had saved me.

"It was dark, and we weren't quite sure where to look, but we began searching anyway. We had been looking for a few minutes, when there was sound. Daniel and I looked at each other and we jumped down on the floor and slid under a bed. A man had come in to get some forgotten object. He looked around for a minute. I can tell you, my little one, I think I stopped breathing for that whole minute. And then I wanted to sneeze. So I pinched my arm. We thought we heard the man leave, but we weren't sure, so we waited. When it was silent, we crawled out. We were both so scared we just ran out of there."

"Did you find the necklace, grandpa?"

"No. We saw a lot of stuff in there. I remember a few nice watches. I think some of the crew had stolen them from passengers. But I couldn't be sure, so we didn't take any. We could have, my little rose, but we weren't thieves. I was in great pain when I went to tell Lily we had failed."

"So Daniel's sister, never got her necklace?"

"Ah, you don't think Lily would give up that easily, do you? This is the girl that beat the Czar. Lily was always thinking. And just like that she came up with a plan."

"What did she do?"

"Lily got a little food. She had Reisel stand not far from Smokes. Then she went up to him, smiled, and offered him the food. He thought maybe he found a little sweetheart. Lily looked much older than her age, but I don't think he cared so much about that anyway."

"What did she say to him? Did she ask if he took it?"

"No. Smokes would just deny he had stolen the necklace. So Lily had to use her Yiddishe kop."

"What's that, grandpa?"

"A Yiddishe kop? That means a Jewish head. She had to be clever to beat this thief. You understand?"

"Yes. But how was she clever?"

"So Lily and the thief talked for a little while. He told her the ship had been in a hurricane on the way back from America last time and all the crew had demanded extra money. She said he was very brave. And so on. All small talk. And then Lily said to him she had a secret and needed his advice. She told him that her friend had given her a gold necklace and she had hidden it in a good place. As she said this she nodded toward Reisel. Suddenly, she said to Smokes, everyone came to her. Now she had three more necklaces to hide, bigger than the first, and worth a lot of money. She told him she was scared. She told him she wanted to know if she should hide these three with the one she had already hidden or in a separate place."

"He wanted to steal those necklaces, too, right, grandpa?"

"Yes, my little rose. He was not just a thief but a greedy thief. Lily knew just what he would think."

My grandfather paused. "Maybe you can guess what the thief was thinking, my little one."

I thought about it. "He had to tell her to hide the necklaces in the same place as the first one because he knew where that was and he could steal them, too."

"Very good, but there's more."

"There is?"

"Yes. Let me give you a hint. He had to tell her to hide it in the same place, but what would she think if she went there and the first necklace was gone?"

"She'd think it was stolen. I've got it, grandpa. He thought he had to put the first necklace back so Lily wouldn't think it was stolen. Then, he thought, she'd put the other three necklaces there and he'd be able to steal all four."

"Ah, my little rose, you have taken up mind reading as a hobby, eh?"

"No, grandpa."

"Well, my sister could read minds, I tell you. So when Smokes told her to wait until the next day and then hide them with the first necklace, she agreed.

"And the next day, she went to the hiding place and found the lost necklace right where it should be. She grabbed it and brought it back to Reisel."

"Lily was smart, wasn't she, grandpa?"

"She was smart, but only for good, my little one."

"And after that, Daniel became your friend?"

"Yes, after that, he trusted me. He knew someone would help him. And we played for the rest of the trip, and we talked for the rest of our lives.

"Wait a minute, grandpa. Dan…I mean Daniel told me that Lily almost saved his sister's life. Did Smokes try to hurt her?"

"No, no. That happened on Ellis Island after we landed."

My grandfather paused for a long while. "I can't tell you what it was like to see the Golden Land, Lily. The men fell down on their knees and prayed. The strong papas and mamas lifted the little children to see it. People who were strangers one minute hugged each other the next. Everyone cried. Everyone."

"Even you, grandpa?"

"A tear or two, yes. This was America. It held all our dreams in its hands. We entered what someone told us was the Narrows and then the Statue of Liberty was on our left. Everyone ran to that side of the ship. We landed, but not on Ellis Island. Then we got on a ferry boat.

"We got off the ferry on Ellis Island. Finally, we were really in America. The man next to me fell down and kissed the earth.

We had been given landing cards which were pinned to our clothes. Everyone was yelling. All I remember is following my mama and papa and going to a big red building. Mama, and Lily, and the baby went into a separate line to see the nurses for the women. Daniel asked papa if he could stay with us. And guess what? Papa told him no, he had to go away."

"He did not, grandpa. Your papa was a nice man."

"No, of course he didn't. You can see right away when I'm kidding. My papa told Daniel not to worry, that he could stay with us and we would watch out for him.

"So we went to get inspected. Remember, we had never seen a doctor or nurse in our whole lives. We were scared. Papa and I walked along. The doctor was in a blue uniform, and he told me to unbutton what I was wearing. I could see when my papa did this he didn't so much like to undress in front of strangers. I was okay until the doctor got to my eyes. He used what felt like a hook to open my eyelid.

"Now, this is the important part. These inspectors put chalk marks on your clothing if you were sick. They used different marks. I saw a lot of the marks, but I didn't know what they meant, except that they were bad. But papa and Daniel and I didn't get a mark. We went to this big hall and sat on benches. We were there for hours. Then they called us up to answer questions. Papa was afraid when they asked him if he had a job waiting in America. But he told the truth and said he didn't. The man looked happy with that answer, which surprised papa.

"When we were finished in the big hall we went down the stairs. Oh that was a sad place."

"Why, grandpa?"

"Because at the bottom of those stairs some people were separated from their families. They were sent to the detention room. The rest of us went along to what they called the kissing post, because relatives of the new immigrants came there to meet those arriving.

"We went along and there was a door with a sign in English. I couldn't read it of course, but I asked, and a man told me it said, 'To New York.'"

"Were grandma and Lily and Yussel okay?"

"They were fine. The problem was with Reisel. I didn't see any of this, but Reisel told us all the story. They came to a nurse. She was young with thin lips, a pretty face, but with demons hiding inside her. She yelled at everyone. She examined mama, took a look at the baby, and then at Lily. It was then Reisel's turn. The nurse said she didn't like the way Reisel looked, that she was too pale. The nurse checked her with some instruments and said she had a problem. Then the nurse took her chalk and made a big "H" chalked on Reisel's coat. That we found out meant she might have a heart problem. It also meant she would be sent back to Europe and Daniel would be all alone."

"Did she have to give the nurse money to let her stay in America?"

My grandfather shrugged. "Who had money for bribes? My family had maybe fifteen dollars left, and that was from what Lily had brought. Reisel had a few dollars, if she had that."

"Then how did she get into America."

"Lily had an idea. They continued walking and when they were out of sight of the nurse Lily told Reisel to exchange coats."

"But that meant Lily had the "H" on her coat."

"Just for a minute, my little rose. Lily took the coat and turned it inside out. Then she put it on. Suddenly there was no "H" on the outside. Suddenly Reisel and Lily were both healthy Americans. And so they came to the kissing post and not to the detention room."

"I wish I could have met Lily."

My grandfather could not move for a minute. Then, in a thick and low voice, he said to me, "You would have liked her very much, and she would have liked you."

"Grandpa, was Reisel really sick?"

"Sick from travel, I think. She got some medicine in New York from Miss Wald on Henry Street. Everyone loved Miss Wald. But that's another story. Anyway, Reisel is still alive. She lives in Florida now with her husband. Every year on the date Lily died, Reisel writes me tear-stained letters. You see, my little one, Reisel knows that if she had been sent back she would have been killed. She knows that Lily saved her life and she doesn't understand a world in which Lily died and she lived. But she donates money in Lily's name to Israel and to the poor and does much good. That's all she can do.

"I'm glad Daniel sells the ice cream."

"I know you are. He had a hard time at the beginning. It was like that for all of us, a struggle. First with the language and the bosses. Then with the anti-Semites. But he worked. Sometimes two jobs. He got married and had three boys, all good boys. And all of them became teachers."

"He's old to be selling ice cream, isn't he grandpa?"

"Yes, he is. Too old. But I left out a sad part of his story. His wife died. A big car hit her one day, and she died. That was a long time ago. And Daniel was very sad. When sadness grabs you it's hard to get free again. But Daniel found a way, my little one. He thought if he made other people happy he would see them smile and then he would be happy again too. And he wondered what would make people happy. He couldn't tell jokes so well. And he couldn't sing or dance. And one day he happened to be walking and saw a group of children waiting for the ice cream truck.

"He watched how excited they were, how their eyes danced just thinking about the ice cream. But then, one little boy began to cry. He had lost his money and was scared to go home and tell his papa.

"So Daniel walked up to the ice cream truck and he paid for the boy to get some ice cream. The little boy stopped crying and said thank you. Daniel said he was welcome. And then he thought of the little boys and girls who didn't have the money for ice cream and he came up with his idea. He would sell ice cream but he would also give it for free to anyone who wanted it. Only he didn't want them to think it was charity, so he came up with the idea of giving them quizzes. This way they studied hard in school so they could be ready for Daniel's quizzes."

"He sells good ice cream."

"He should sell stuff that tastes like when I cook? He'd only sell good stuff."

"Mama says if I eat too much ice cream I'll get fat like Uncle Marvin."

"Everyone has to eat ice cream sometimes, my little one. It's okay."

And to this day whenever I think back to my own children buying ice cream, I remember the smiles on their faces. I think of their great-grandfather. But mostly I wish there had been a Dan, the Ice Cream Man for them

CHAPTER FOUR:
THE LAND OF EIGHTEEN DREAMS

"You look like all the troubles in the world came for a visit."

I was eating breakfast in the tiny alcove off the kitchen in my grandfather's apartment. My parents were at a convention in the Catskills, and I had stayed overnight with my grandparents.

I wasn't sure whether to tell my grandfather about it or not. This was private. But then I thought maybe he could help. I knew somebody had to help.

Finally, the words just tumbled out. "Grandpa, you know my friend, Katie Kelly?"

"Sure. She's the one with the leg brace."

"Grandpa! That's all anyone sees. They make fun of her limp."

"I'm sorry, Lily. You're right. She's a nice girl, right?"

"Very nice. We do our homework together. And we tell each other what books to read. Only now she's in trouble."

"And your face tells me you want to help."

"I do. And I promised I would. But I'm not sure I can because I'm so scared."

"So, let's hear it. Sometimes even when you say it out loud you get an idea."

I nodded. "All the boys were teasing her because she walks so slow. Then they dared her to walk through Hitler's Cave."

My grandfather, who had by then sat down opposite me, look startled. "What is this, Hitler's Cave?"

"It's a big tunnel in a basement. The boys have Cub Scout meetings on one side, but on the other is this long, dark tunnel. Everyone is scared to go through. They say Hitler is waiting in there to catch little children."

"You know that's silly. Hitler's dead."

"I know it. But it's scary. And it really is dark. Anyway, Katie said she would do it. And she couldn't just lie because the boys said there's writing on a wall at the end and she has to tell them what it says.

"So yesterday she started to walk through the cave and didn't get far when she screamed and got really scared. Now she can't go in again."

"And she doesn't want to tell the boys."

"No, grandpa. They'd make fun of her even more." I paused. "So last night I promised Katie I'd walk through Hitler's Cave this morning and tell her what was on the wall so she could say she walked through it. Only now, I'm really, really scared."

"Ah. It's a nice day for a walk. Come I'll walk through this cave with you. And if we run into Hitler, believe me I know what to do to him."

I looked up. "Really, grandpa, you'll come with me?"

"Sure. When I was young I went into the dark mines under the earth. All right, only once, but I went."

"Aren't you scared?"

"A smart person is always a little scared, Lily, but a smart person keeps going anyway. You finish your breakfast, and we'll do it right now before we both get too scared."

"Okay, grandpa."

And so we walked a few blocks over to the basement of an apartment building. The door to the basement creaked as my grandpa pushed it open. Even the hall which usually had lights on was dark.

"So where is Hitler hiding out in here?"

"This way, grandpa." The cub scouts met in the room on the left and the passageway on the right was the beginning of what we called the cave.

My grandfather had taken a flashlight, and he put it on so we could see that entrance. We began walking. My mouth was dry. I was listening for every sound. I was scared somebody would grab me.

"You know, my little rose, this is dark just like the tenement building where I first lived when my family got to the Lower East Side."

"It was dark like this, grandpa?"

"Like this, but with stairs we had to climb every day. Listen, my little rose, do you mind if I tell you the story of that tenement? It will help me be less scared of the dark."

"Sure. Go ahead, grandpa."

"Good. So America was very strange. We had never seen chewing gum. There was so much I hadn't seen. And I was a greenie, a newcomer. I believed people because I thought this wasn't Russia anymore. Once a neighbor boy told me Old Man Kirshenbaum had a magic coffee grinder in his store that could turn pennies into gold. So one day I tried it. It didn't work, and then neither did the coffee grinder. I had to work for a long time in the store to pay for that.

"My mama was a miracle worker. We didn't have much money, so my mama had to be careful when she shopped. Why, Lily, my mama could go to a store and look a carp in the eye and tell you the day it died. She knew if it had a cloudy eye it wasn't fresh.

"But once I got sick, a fever, and even mama didn't know what to do. Well, there were visiting nurses who came over from Henry Street, from a place Miss Wald had started. They took care of all the sick children in the neighborhood. You should have seen those nurses, my little one. They walked on the roofs when they were in a hurry because the streets were too crowded. God alone knows how many lives they saved. Mine included. I was very sick. And the nurse came and made me better. We didn't have any money, but she said Miss Wald had gotten money from other Jews and she would take care of me even if I couldn't pay. We called Miss Wald The Angel of Henry Street.

"And school. Oh, that was something. I got put in a class with the little children because I couldn't speak or write English. Even the seats were tiny. Let me tell you that made me want to learn fast. But I liked school, especially our music teacher. She was very good, but she only knew one song. It was called 'When You Were Sweet Sixteen.' Every class, that's all she played. When President McKinley died, we were the only school in America to march in to an assembly to the tune of 'When You Were Sweet Sixteen.'

"I was good in school, but my mama wanted me to be especially good in English, so I got some help from our boarder. He made me love English."

"What's a boarder, grandpa?"

"We didn't have much money, so we rented in a tenement on Rivington Street. Oy. So small. All the people used to say we had plenty of everything, plenty of noise, plenty of dirt, plenty of hunger. But this apartment. It was tiny. There was a room in back for mama and papa. I slept in the front room, which was called the parlor, along with my sister and the baby. Papa didn't make so much money, so in exchange for some money we let other people stay in our apartment, even though it was tiny. These people who stayed were called boarders.

"I don't know the name of the boarder who helped me with English because we only called him by his nickname, Yankel Shakespeare."

"That's a funny name, grandpa."

"He was a great poet. Or he thought he was. So papa took four empty herring barrels and he set them up in a rectangle.

Then he put a spring on the barrels and we had a bed for our poet boarder."

"Did you like Yankel Shakespeare, grandpa?"

"Oh, very much. He always had stories for me. And every Jewish holiday he wrote poems for everyone in the building, including that nogoodnik, Meyer Cohen, may his name be cursed. This Cohen was our landlord, and every Friday morning he came to collect the rent. He lived in one of the apartments with a wife that, well I won't speak so ill of her because she had to live with Cohen. And they had four nice daughters, including the sweetest one, Shoshi.

"Anyway, Yankel wrote all these poems. And he gave them to everyone, even Cohen. Yankel was very good at writing poems. Unfortunately, he was better at this writing than he was at getting jobs. So he couldn't pay his rent."

"Maybe we should have told him to leave so we could get a boarder who could pay, but my mama said that Yankel was a nice young man, and it's not his fault if people didn't appreciate him. He always looked very hard for work and worked hard when he got a job. But his mind was always in the sky, mama said.

"So mama one day announced that she had made a deal with Yankel. He would help me with my English in return for his stay…"

My grandfather stopped talking because there was a strange sound in the cave.

"What's that, grandpa?"

"A bird maybe."

"You don't think it's a wild animal, do you? Or…somebody?"

"Whatever it is, we'll be all right, my little one. I'll sock it with this flashlight."

"It's a long cave, grandpa."

"That it is. But not as long as our courage, my little one."

"I guess so."

We kept walking. I looked in every shadow. Two boys had told me they had seen Hitler hiding in the shadows. I shivered.

After a minute of quiet my grandfather began speaking again.

"So Yankel taught me English. Only he taught it to me in a funny way. He made me learn his poems in Yiddish and then made me translate them into English. I still remember those poems, especially my favorite. It was called 'The Land of Eighteen Dreams.'"

"Did he make you say it?"

"My mama did. Every night I had to recite a new poem in English. I don't think she understood what I was saying, but she always nodded and smiled because her little boy spoke English like an American."

"My teacher made us memorize a poem by Edgar Allan Poe, grandpa."

"It's fun, isn't it?"

"Yes. I like the sounds in the poems."

"And I loved to recite 'The Land of Eighteen Dreams.'"

"Why did Yankel call it that, grandpa?"

"For a couple of reasons. First, each of the Hebrew letters has a special meaning and is given a number. The letters that make up the word 'life' in Hebrew add up to eighteen, so it's an important number.

"And there was another reason. Yankel said everyone who came to America had eighteen dreams, that America was the land of eighteen dreams. These eighteen dreams together added up to a new beginning, to life."

"Do you still remember the eighteen dreams, grandpa?"

"Sure. I can tell you all of them. Do you want to hear?"

I got my fingers ready. "Yes. You can begin, grandpa."

"The dreams that all newcomers to America had were for gold in the streets, freedom, love, a warm home, beautiful children, many friends, undeserved luck, a shining face, a good voice, a quick mind, the chance to laugh often, a splendid heart, a big library, a soft bed, a place to walk, leaders who care about people, and a partnership with God."

"Grandpa! I was counting with my fingers. That was only seventeen dreams."

"Ah, my little rose. Always with the numbers. I'm walking in the dark with a nine year old Einstein."

"So what was the eighteenth dream, grandpa?"

"The eighteenth dream was a private one. All people have to decide for themselves what that eighteenth dream is. It's different for each person. The task of life for all of us was to look for that eighteenth dream in our lives. And it is in America that we could look because we were free here."

"That's a good poem, grandpa."

"I thought so. Only I also thought poems don't pay the rent. As I really found out one Friday morning when papa didn't have the rent money.

"Oh, my little one. It was so cold and wet that day. And that wicked man Meyer Cohen evicted us, sent us out on the sidewalk in the rain. There we were with all we owned sitting in front of the tenement as the sky cried on us. Mama set up a little plate, and some people gave pennies. If we had enough by sunset we could get back into the apartment for Shabbos.

"Mama held the baby, while Papa, my sister, and I went out looking for money. I went to where the new immigrants came in and brought some to a tenement on Delancey Street. There was a man there who gave me some money if I brought people to him and they rented in his tenement. Many places gave free rent at first, but not him. He wanted money right from the start. Anyway, I found some people, but my bad luck they didn't have any money for rent. Then I spent another two hours until I found a family with money. Then it took me time to bring them over to the tenement. I thought the day was cursed because there were no apartments for rent.

"I almost cried."

"Did you think of stealing some money, grandpa?"

"Sure. But I couldn't. I once went to get my sister from her work. She had gotten her pay, and told her boss there was a quarter missing. He knew she was honest so he gave her the quarter. Then we started walking home, and she discovered the quarter she thought was lost. So she said we had to walk all the way back to her work to return the quarter she had taken by mistake from her boss. In my family, we didn't steal. A friend of mine was a doorman for some gamblers, but I didn't want to be like him."

"He opened doors for the gamblers, grandpa?"

"No, no. He kept a look out for the police. And if they were coming he warned the gamblers. He wasn't going to be arrested because he was too young. But I didn't want to do that.

"So there I was, my little one. With no money walking very slowly back home."

I was going to ask my grandfather what happened to his family, but we had reached the end of the cave.

We stopped. "Thanks, grandpa. It was okay walking with you."

"You're welcome, Lily. It was okay walking with you, too."

"We have to find the writing, grandpa."

"I know." He began swinging the flashlight from side to side. And then, scrawled in fading blue paint on one of the walls were the words, "Hitler's looking for you."

My grandfather just stood there. "These are words the people who hated us yelled when there was a war in Europe, and they didn't want America to fight. Those words still hurt me."

"I'm sorry, grandpa."

"I know you are. Now you know the words to tell, Katie."

"Yes, grandpa, only I'll tell her to say they were bad words."

"That they are. Come, Lily, you have done your good deed. It is time to go back to the land of the living."

We walked in silence for a while. I could tell that my grandfather felt very sad, so I said to him, "Grandpa you have to finish the story."

"Ah, you want to know what happened. As I said, it was a long walk back home. I remember every sight, the organ grinder, the dead horse lying in the street, I can see them all. Believe me, I didn't want to go home. I wanted to go to Hubert's Museum on 14th Street and look at the trained fleas.

"When I arrived home, papa and my sister were there, and I could tell by the look on their faces that they did not have enough money. They looked at me, and I had to shake my head. I was so ashamed. I had let my family down. But they just nodded. I sat down.

"I asked my papa how much we still needed. He told me we still needed six dollars. He might have said a million dollars. Where were we going to get six dollars? There was only a little while to go. I thought we'd be living on the street that night, my little one. And then came the miracle."

"You found some money in the street, grandpa?"

"No, no. This was the miracle of love."

"What happened, grandpa?"

"It wasn't five minutes after I sat down when Yankel Shakespeare came running out of the tenement screaming. He was waving a ten dollar bill and yelling that he had the money. He gave it to papa. I tell you Lily to this day I do not know how my mama did it, but somehow we were eating some chicken in our apartment for Shabbos dinner."

"But how did Yankel Shakespeare get the money, grandpa?"

"Remember that Yankel always gave poems to everyone? Well Shoshi Cohen, the landlord's sweet daughter, learned all the poems by heart. When she heard what her father did to us, she hired Yankel Shakespeare to write a poem about her. And then when he did she paid him $10 for the poem. He was the highest paid poet in America, I can tell you that."

"What happened to Yankel?"

"Yankel and Shoshi got married. What else could they do? He had written poetry for her. So Yankel became our neighbor and not our boarder. But you know what, my little one? He kept teaching me English and giving me books to read."

We had reached the entrance. It was good to walk outside. The light was blinding for a second, but I felt so relieved that the walk through the cave was over and that I could tell Katie what was on the wall.

We began walking. My grandfather led us to the luncheonette on the corner of 21st Avenue and 79th Street.

"Come, Lily, we need a reward."

We went inside and sat down at the soda fountain. Mr. Belzer, who owned the luncheonette, walked over and said hello. I ordered a chocolate ice cream soda with coffee ice cream. My grandfather ordered the same. Mr. Belzer's face looked gray to me, and he always seemed sad. But he smiled at my grandfather and me and walked over to make the ice cream sodas.

Then my grandfather gave me a coin and said, "Here, Lily, go call your nice friend and tell her you have walked through the valley of the shadow of death."

I ran off and made the call and then returned to sit down.

"Katie was crying because she was so happy, grandpa. She says to say thank you."

"This is a polite little girl. Very nice."

"She is very nice, grandpa. Always. She said she is going to take a bath and get dressed. Then she's coming over to your apartment. We're going to see the boys. Her brother told her they are playing in the yard at P.S. 2. Are they going to be surprised."

We sat for a few moments in silence. I don't recall any ice cream soda I've ever had in my life that tasted so good.

Then I turned to my grandfather and said, "Grandpa, I know what my eighteenth dream in America is."

"What's that, my little rose?"

"My eighteenth dream is that you never go away."

I'm not sure, but I think I saw a tear at the corner of his eye. I'd never seen my grandfather crying, so I couldn't be certain. When he spoke, though, his voice was thick.

"That's very nice of you, Lily, but a dream can't control what happens to another person, only to you. You have to dream for yourself."

"Then I dream I'll grow up to be just like you."

"Maybe without the beard."

"Yes, grandpa. I'll skip that part."

"Good idea. Only dream a bigger dream for yourself. Don't come to the ocean of hope with a tiny thimble. Come with a huge pail. And don't worry if it takes a long time to figure it out. Sometimes people don't even know their true eighteenth dream until they're old."

We finished our ice cream sodas, and my grandfather and I walked home.

Later, Katie did come over and we did walk over to see the boys who had made fun of her. She was beaming when she talked. She described the walk in the cave to them as I had described it to her. Earlier I had told her that it was okay to say she had done it, that my grandfather called such statements a higher truth.

The boys crowded around. They were suspicious, surprised she knew the words, slow to be nice to her. But she was proud as she stood there and told them the story. Later, when the other boys were gone, one boy came over to her and said he was sorry. She nodded, thanking him.

Katie and I have stayed in touch across the decades. One year not long ago, just before Rosh Hashanah, she asked to go with me to visit my grandfather's grave. She had married and had three children and always looked happy when I saw her except for when we got to the grave.

We placed a few pebbles on it and then stood still. Katie was very silent. When she finished, she turned to me and said, "I was thanking him for giving me a new life."

I told her that my grandfather had given her the eighteenth dream. She asked me what I meant and on the drive back I told her.

As for me, I've thought long and hard about what my eighteenth dream should be. It did take me a long time to discover it.

Finally, though, years later, I found it.

But that's another story.

CHAPTER FIVE:
THE GALLERY OF MISSING HUSBANDS

"You have to invite her. It's your tenth birthday, and she's your friend and your neighbor. What would her mother think of me if you don't invite her?"

"I'm not going to. If you make me invite her, I'm not going to have a birthday party at all."

My mother was not going to back down on this, I knew. But I couldn't tell her the truth.

I raised my voice. "Grandpa doesn't celebrate his birthday. Why do I have to celebrate mine?"

She stepped toward me. "Your grandfather is a wonderful man. But on this he's crazy. Whoever heard of not celebrating your birthday because other people are sad that someone they know died on that date? That makes no sense of all."

"I just want to be like grandpa, that's all."

"So be like him. Right after your birthday party."

I ran out of the apartment and went to the bench in the back where I always went.

My grandfather trudged along about twenty minutes later.

I looked up at him.

"She made you come here, didn't she?"

"At this very moment I'm supposed to be yelling at you."

"You're not doing a very good job."

"What's the matter, Lily? Why don't you want this little girl, Karen, to come to your party?"

"I did something bad, grandpa."

"I don't understand. You did something bad to your friend?"

"No."

"You don't want to say?"

"No."

I thought my grandfather would argue with me. Or tell me I could talk to him. But he sat silently on the bench beside me. We both stared ahead.

"You feel guilty, Lily?"

"I guess so. I don't want to talk about it, grandpa."

His voice was almost a whisper. "I understand. Sometimes we keep such secrets wrapped up inside us so tight it hurts."

He was quiet again. I was surprised because my grandfather didn't usually sit in silence. I looked over at him. His face looked a little twisted. I thought maybe I had hurt his feelings and was about to talk with him when he spoke.

"Lily, it's not good to keep such guilt inside. I do it, and it hurts every year on my birthday."

"But you don't celebrate your birthday, grandpa."

"There's a reason I don't celebrate, a real one, not the one I say. Maybe if I tell you, it will help a bit. You'll see, my secret is much worse than yours, Lily, much worse, whatever yours is."

"You did something bad, grandpa?"

"Something terrible. So bad I don't ever speak about it."

"But grandpa you're a nice man."

"Not so nice, Lily. At least I wasn't once. Can I tell you the story?"

"Sure, grandpa. I won't tell anyone."

He nodded. "Good. And remember. I'm only telling it so you'll see what you did isn't so bad.

"I was nineteen years old. I already had a lot of jobs, mostly delivering, also working in shops. But Abe Cahan gave me the job that mattered."

"Who was he?"

"Cahan was the editor of the *Forward*, a Yiddish newspaper, the one most people read. Oh, he was a tyrant, always yelling at the reporters that their writing was too fancy, that they should write so people understood them. Or he yelled they weren't American enough. He was a dictator, I can tell you that. But the readers loved him. And I loved him, because he gave me a start in journalism.

"He hired me to do some reporting on the East Side. I went to the market on Hester Street Thursday nights. I interviewed the marriage brokers, the people who made egg creams, the seltzer delivery people, the matchmakers, the rabbis, everybody who would talk to me.

"And then, one day, Cahan told me he liked my writing, and he wanted me to add another part to my job. Besides writing, he wanted me to help people with The Gallery of Missing Husbands."

"You were a detective, grandpa?"

"No, no. I helped the women write ads. Cahan thought I needed to meet more kinds of people to help my writing. So he had me meet them and learn their stories. There was a big problem, then, Lily. Husbands sometimes left their families and went away. So Cahan thought his paper should publish photographs of the missing men in case anyone knew where they were. And women had ads with the photograph, begging readers to help them find the missing husbands. I helped write the ads. That's all. Or I thought that was all.

"One day, a woman walked into the office. Someone sent her to me, and she said she needed help because she didn't know how to write so well. We talked and I wrote the ad. It's the ad that has stuck with me all this time."

"Was she very young?"

"She was almost thirty. She came in with a little boy named Theodore. He must have been born around the time Theodore Roosevelt became president. He was maybe seven years old. I smiled at him, but he didn't smile back at me."

He stopped, leaned forward, and took his wallet out of his pocket. He opened it and pulled out a yellowed piece of paper. "Here's the ad I wrote, Lily."

I held the paper delicately and read: "Rina Solomon is looking for her husband Nathan, age 32, medium height, big build, brown beard. The little finger of his left hand is bent. He left me and my boy a year ago. Whoever knows of him should have mercy on us and notify me at 132 Ludlow Street in the restaurant."

"It's very sad, grandpa."

"So I thought. And she was so pretty. And I was a young man, so I was sorry for her. And I made the mistake a lot of young men make when they see a pretty woman. I made a promise.

"I told the young woman that I would find her husband. I thought, I'm a reporter. I can go places, ask questions. How hard can it be to find this Nathan Solomon?"

"Did you find him, grandpa?"

"Before I tell you Lily, why don't you tell me about your problem?"

I considered that. "Grandpa, you won't like me if I tell you."

"That's not possible, Lily. No matter what you did I will love you even if I don't like what you did."

"Promise?"

"I promise."

"Okay, but remember you promised. " I paused. "Karen and I were in Mr. Kleinman's 5 & 10 cent store where I buy button candy. We were walking down an aisle when Karen picked a toy off the shelf. Mr. Kleinman was talking with some people and didn't see us. Karen snapped the toy. And then another. And other. Three toys, grandpa.

"Did you break any, Lily?"

"No, of course not, grandpa."

"Okay, so what happened next?"

"Karen just walked out of the store like she had done nothing wrong."

I looked down. "I didn't tell Mr. Kleinman, grandpa. He is a nice man. I buy the button candy just about every day after school, and once I came in and I didn't have any money. I just went to look at the candy. And he asked me why I kept staring at those little candy buttons. I told him, and he gave me some. He was nice to me, and I was mean to him because I didn't tell him. Karen was my friend and I couldn't get my friend in trouble."

"Those toys cost him money, Lily."

"I know. And I know I should have told him. That's what I did wrong, grandpa. I didn't tell him or mama or papa or anybody."

"Why did little Karen do this?"

"I don't know. She was mad at her mother, I know that."

"Maybe she only did it once, Lily, so she learned. Maybe she saw that you didn't break a toy and she learned what to do from you. That's what it means to be sorry, to face the same temptation you gave into and then resist it."

"You're just trying to make me feel better, grandpa. But we went back into the store the next day and she broke two more toys. That made five. She doesn't take things. She breaks them. That's why I don't want to invite her to my birthday party, only I can't tell mama the real reason."

"This is a problem."

"Maybe Karen will move away."

"I don't think she's moving so fast. You'll have to solve this for yourself. But maybe if we talk it over we can come up with a way. Let me think about it."

"While you're thinking, grandpa, tell me if you ever found Nathan Solomon."

59

"Okay. Well, I started in right away. I looked uptown, downtown. I took his picture all over."

"I didn't even know they had pictures then."

"Sure. Why there were photographers on the streets who would take your picture and put it on a button."

"I wish they had those now, grandpa. I'd take a picture of you and me."

"Ah, I'm afraid my face would ruin the picture, my little one."

"No it wouldn't. And you still haven't told me if you found him."

"No, I didn't, not then. I gave up. For the next part I have to tell you about my sister, Lily. She had gone to work in a photographers' studio on Second Avenue. She was just a secretary, but part of her job was to deliver the photos to the stars in the Yiddish theater. Everybody loved those stars. The people hung on their every word. The stars right from the stage would invite audiences to their weddings. They'd complain about their husband or wife during a performance. They did a Shakespeare play and people in the audience yelled for the author.

"Everyone loved Lily, of course. One day she arrived with the pictures, when the director grabbed her. He told her one of the actresses was out sick. He meant she was drunk again, but he was too polite to say. He knew Lily had memorized the lines, and he begged her to go on the stage.

"Lily was in heaven. It was a dream for her. She got up there and didn't make a single mistake. Right there the director hired her."

"Was Lily a star?"

"She was no Molly Picon, but she was popular."

"Did she know Nathan Solomon, grandpa?"

"I'm coming to that."

"Oh."

"One day, a young man walks into the Yiddish theater."

"Not Nathan Solomon?"

"No, no. Not Nathan Solomon. Who's telling this story anyway?"

"Sorry, grandpa."

"All right. So in walks a man His name is Izzy Feldman, he tells her, but he calls himself Jimmy Stanton, like the street name. Jimmy Stanton had started in the Yiddish theater but he worked in vaudeville. Everybody changed their names then."

"Was it because he was Jewish?"

"No, it was out of respect for his family. Everybody thought vaudeville was not so kosher, and he didn't want to disgrace his family."

"What's vaudeville, grandpa?"

"It was like a variety show, like what Ed Sullivan does on Sunday nights on television. There were lots of different acts, something for everyone, only it was live on stage."

"Was Jimmy Stanton a singer?"

"Jimmy Stanton was everything. They needed a juggler, he was juggler. They needed somebody with a trained seal he rented a seal and had an act. He did very well for a while with a mutt in an act he called 'The Wonder Dog and His Helper.' I told him he wasn't doing so great if the dog got top billing. Finally, he became a comic. Not a funny comic, but a comic.

"He wanted Lily to become his woman partner in the act. He showed her some of what she had written, and he made her laugh.

"She agreed to try. They didn't do so well at first. They were called a disappointment act. That meant when another act didn't show up, a manager would call them and they'd hop on a train and go to the place. They went all over.

"I didn't like Jimmy very much. He said being Jewish had been bad for him, that it made him guilty about having any pleasure, and that he had to unlearn being Jewish to enjoy himself. Oh, he liked to drink a lot of wine. And eat all the forbidden foods. Every food, really. And a lot of it. And Jimmy Stanton would make any bet. Why if he were sitting here right now, he'd bet you ten dollars that we'd see a dog within five minutes. Crazy stuff like that. He lost a lot of money betting.

"I told him that the greatest pleasure in the world is to do what's right. But he didn't want to hear me. I told him he should be the master of his will and the servant of his conscience. He told me to go back to the Old Country.

"I didn't like his being friends with my sister. But she said they were just partners in an act, that she liked being around him, that she loved being in vaudeville. It was Jimmy who had the idea about Nathan Solomon. After I told him the story and showed him the picture, he said that he'd take it to every town he went to play. And that was just about any town there was in the area.

"It took almost four months, but Jimmy called me one day and told me that he had showed the photo to people in Albany, and they recognized Nathan Solomon. He was still going by that name. Jimmy asked me if he should talk to Solomon, but I said not to, that I would take a train up there and speak to him myself.

"And that's where the trouble started. I took a train to Albany, talked with the person Jimmy spoke with, learned where Nathan Solomon worked, and went to a shop. I walked in, and I immediately recognized him.

"I confronted him. I told him I knew who he was, that he had abandoned his wife and son, and that I demanded he return to them."

"Did you get into a fight with him?"

"No, my little one. He was very calm. He said we should go to a restaurant and talk. We sat down, ordered our food, and then he told me his story.

"He admitted running away. He said I didn't know that his wife had given birth to a daughter six months before he left but that the daughter had died in a fire as an infant."

"That's horrible, grandpa."

"I know. It's just what happened so I have to tell you. The mama slipped and the infant fell on the stove. Oh, it's too terrible, Lily. I can't talk about any more details.

"So the man was telling me this story. He began to cry. He said his wife was not the same again, that she couldn't get over it. I said then he was even worse, leaving his wife after she had gone through that. He said I was right, but he just couldn't take it. She screamed when he went to kiss her. She screamed in the morning and at night. She screamed at their boy. All the time she screamed. He told her to get help, but she didn't.

"Then after a while, he told me he couldn't stand to listen to her. And one day, without planning, he just got up, boarded the train to Albany, and didn't come back.

"We talked for a long while. Then he brought me to meet a woman. It was the woman he loved, he said, and who loved him. I could see that she was pregnant.

"He begged me to let him start again, that if he left now he would be abandoning this woman and a newborn. That he and the woman and the new baby all needed each other.

"I didn't know what to do, Lily. All that night I walked around Albany. I sat in a park and I thought. And then the next day I took the train back to New York and went to see Rina Solomon. I looked right at her and lied. I told her that I couldn't find her husband. I let her stay abandoned, and I let her son grow up without a father."

"It was just as I returned after speaking with her that some people in the newspaper office came up to me and wished me a happy birthday. But it wasn't so happy for me. Every year when other people celebrate on their birthdays, I spend mine thinking of the woman I lied to and the boy I let down. I would have hurt one woman or another, but I only broke a promise to one of them. How can I celebrate my birthday when every year I remember doing that?"

"But why did you do it, grandpa?"

My grandfather sighed. "I was so mixed up. I told myself that Nathan wouldn't go back even if I told his wife where he was. And Rina and the boy would know he had another family, which would make them feel even worse. Not telling seemed like the choice that would cause the least hurt to everyone. I don't know about the others, but it didn't stop hurting me."

There was more silence until I finally asked, "What are we going to do, grandpa?"

"I don't know what I'm going to do about me, but I know what you should do, my little one."

"You do? What's that?"

"First, you have to decide if you think your friend will break things again if you go to a store with her."

I nodded. "I'm sure she will."

"Okay, then you have to tell her that you don't want to be her friend anymore, and she has to tell her mother that she doesn't want to go to your party, or you'll tell her mother what happened."

"It's not so easy to find a friend, grandpa."

"No, it isn't. But it's easy to find someone who's not a good friend."

"What should I do about the store? I thought of doing what you did with the coffee grinder and working in the store until I paid back what the toys cost, but then Mr. Kleinman would ask me who did it, and I can't lie. So I can't do that."

"I know that too." And he told me what to do. Then he gave me some money. I went over to see Karen, and then I got a sweater like my grandfather said, walked over and went into the store twice.

When I returned, I was still eating the button candy. I thanked my grandfather and I said, "Grandpa, what happened to the little boy, Rina Solomon's son?"

"I don't know."

"You said he was seven years old, much younger than you. He must still be alive."

"You think I should look for him?"

"Don't you want to know, grandpa?"

"I'm not sure. I'm curious, but I don't want to cause him more hurt by telling him now what I didn't tell him then."

"But he's big now. He should know the truth."

I could see my grandfather didn't want to do it, but he finally said, "You're right, my little one. He deserves to know. Come on, let's look."

We walked back to his apartment and looked in the Manhattan phone book. There was one person listed. My grandfather called him and asked if he was Rina Solomon's son. But he wasn't the right man.

"Maybe he moved like you did, grandpa."

"Maybe. But he could be anywhere. It's a common enough name. Still, you've gotten me interested."

He looked in the Queens directory, and again there was one name.

He was the right Theodore Solomon.

I watched my grandfather's face as he talked on the phone. At one point I thought he was going to collapse. I ran to get a chair for him. He asked me for a glass of water. Three times he wiped his eyes with the back of his hand.

When he finished, he walked over to the kitchen table and put his head down in his arms. I let him sit there for several minutes. Then I said, "Can I get you anything, grandpa?"

He shook his head.

"What happened, grandpa?"

It took him even more time until he was ready. "At first he said he wanted to meet and not speak on the phone. And then I think all the hurt opened up, and he was the one who wanted to speak, who needed to speak. Lily, he wanted to thank me."

My grandfather stopped for a few seconds.

"It's a sad story. His mama went crazy, and they locked her up. Theodore went to a children's asylum, but a nice Jewish couple from the Upper East Side took him in. He said they raised him as their son.

"He's a photographer, now, taking all kinds of pictures."

"Was he mad at you grandpa?"

"No, and I'll tell you why. Right after I spoke with Nathan Solomon, Nathan came back to see the family. He begged their forgiveness but said he couldn't return permanently. And he couldn't take his son because the woman in Albany didn't know about this other family.

"So what he did was call friends. It was one of his friends who had a boss. This boss and his wife couldn't have children."

"They're the ones who took in Theodore?"

"Yes. Nathan Solomon arranged it, and knew all about what Theodore was doing. After his father died, Theodore checked on the child in Albany. He was a man by then, and the two stayed in touch. That man in Albany died two years ago.

"Theodore forgave me because if I hadn't gone to see his father, he was sure Nathan never would have returned, and wouldn't have made arrangements for him to be taken care of by that couple.

"I asked if he hated his father, and he said great words of wisdom to me. He said, 'How do you hate somebody who's heartbroken?'"

I had a very nice birthday party that year. Karen didn't attend. She and I continued to nod or say hello to each other, but we stopped being friends. I don't know what happened to her.

A little more than a month after my birthday, at the end of October, my grandfather celebrated his birthday for the first time in almost half a century. Everyone had a great time, but they wondered why he had begun celebrating his birthday again. And they also wanted to know why he had hired a photographer to take so many pictures at the party. The family got used to the photographer because he returned every year after that on my grandfather's birthday.

I look at those pictures each year on his birthday. When they were young, I told my own children this story. And at the end, even when they knew, they always asked me what had happened in the store, what had I done about the broken toys.

And I told them. I took my grandfather's money, went to the store, and used most of it to buy five toys, the same number and the same toys Karen had broken. I went to the front of the store and paid for them. Then I went outside, waited ten minutes, and went into the store a second time. I hid the five toys under my sweater, which I carried over my arm. I took the toys to the shelf where I had bought them and put them all back.

I used the rest of the money to buy some button candy and smiled as I walked home.

CHAPTER SIX:
THE DAY OF ATONEMENT

"Grandpa, I think I killed Dennis Bello."

My grandfather was sitting outside despite the breeze looking at the weeping willow tree in the apartment building's front yard. There was a book folded across his chest.

He turned to look at me. "I thought he's just in the hospital, Lily. You didn't kill anybody."

"He is in the hospital. Only no one knows what happened except for me. And I'm afraid he's going to die."

"He has very good doctors."

"I guess so, grandpa."

"And they're operating tomorrow. So I don't think there's a lot you can do, Lily."

"Should I pray for him, grandpa, even if I'm not so sure I believe in prayer?"

"If it makes you feel better."

"But will it help him? I'll promise anything to God if Dennis gets better."

"I don't know if it will help him, my little one."

He stood up. "Lily, if I thought God had the power to make Dennis better, then I have to say he had to power to stop Dennis from getting hurt in the first place but didn't do it."

"I don't understand, grandpa."

"We should both hope the doctors have the wisdom and strength to help Dennis. Is that okay?"

"That's good, grandpa."

"Okay. So now, tell me what you think you did."

"Can I show you, grandpa? It's in the back yard, by the fort."

In the land behind my apartment buildings there was a space between other buildings on the left and right. There was a place where the boys played baseball, and a big oak tree and, on a hill, the remains of the foundation of a house that was never built. We called that white stone foundation the fort, and we played games from it. Some of us would stand in the fort and some of us would stand at the bottom of the hill.

We threw rocks at each other. Not pebbles, but rocks. They weren't huge, because then we couldn't throw them, but they were big. I don't remember how this game started, but we played it every few weeks, especially in the summer. I had the vague feeling that we shouldn't throw rocks at each other, but I joined with the others.

My grandfather walked slowly, and I went beside him. He waved to some of the children on the block who waved back at him. We got to the hill at the bottom of the fort.

"Okay, Lily. What happened?"

I pointed. "I was right up there, grandpa. In the front of the fort on the right side. We were throwing rocks at each other."

He looked down at me. "That's very bad, Lily."

"I know, but we did it all the time and nobody ever got hurt before."

"You were all just lucky."

"Nobody thought about it."

"Okay, so you were up there throwing rocks."

"Yes, grandpa. I have a good aim. I practice with trees. But I wasn't aiming at anyone. Really, I wasn't. I just threw the rocks for fun. I thought they'd land somewhere on the ground."

"And Dennis got hit."

"Yes, grandpa. In his right eye." I started to cry. "He was bleeding very bad, grandpa, very bad. I just sat beside him and someone went to tell his mother."

"I don't understand, Lily. You didn't aim at him. Other children were throwing rocks, yes?"

"Yes, there were five of us in the fort."

"So why do you think it was your rock that hit Dennis?"

"Because he got hit a few seconds after I threw it. I just know I did it, grandpa. But I was afraid to tell anyone else. And now he's going to die. Are they going to put me in jail, grandpa? I don't want to go to jail."

"No, Lily. Jail is for bad people, not you. But what you did was still not right whether you hit him or not."

I sniffed a few times. "I just don't know what to do, grandpa. I want to make up for what I did, but I don't know how."

"I want t tell you a story, Lily. It is about the man my sister Lily was going to marry."

"Was it the comedian she was going to marry? The one she had an act with?"

"No, no. Jimmy Stanton was the comedian. He and Lily had an act, and it didn't do so well. Jimmy was very much in love with my sister. Every day he bought her a flower or some chocolates or sent her a telegram. Every day he asked her to marry him, but she didn't want to because she didn't think he was the best sort of person.

"Come, let's sit down, Lily."

We walked over to a bench. When we were seated, my grandfather continued his story.

"My sister kept refusing him, and Jimmy finally got angry. One day, it was my sister's birthday, he gave her a big present, an expensive diamond, and he said either she had to marry him or she was out of the act.

"This was very difficult for my sister because she loved vaudeville. And if she wasn't the greatest talent in show business, she enjoyed telling the jokes on stage and singing a little bit. For a servant girl this was a big step up in the world.

"Her friends told her she was old, that she wouldn't find another man, and that Jimmy was funny and bound to be successful one day because he really wanted it.

"But my sister just couldn't do it. She told Jimmy goodbye. He stormed out of her apartment."

"He let her into the act again, didn't he, grandpa?"

"No, he didn't. He meant it. But he recovered. Instead of spending money on flowers and candy, he hired a writer to make up the jokes in the act. He decided not to use a woman partner, so he just stood there by himself telling jokes. And then he developed a personality audiences recognized. That's what the writer told him to do. More and more, Jimmy became famous.

"But Lily didn't care. She knew she had been right. And then, one day, she was sitting on East Houston Street having a knish in Yonah Schimmel's bakery. And there was not much room. A stranger had to sit right beside her. He apologized, and she said it was fine. She could see he was religious, but he was reading an American book. He looked over and saw she was reading a book by the same writer, and he asked if she liked the writer.

"And she began to speak. Let me tell you, my sister could talk."

"Grandma says you can talk, too, grandpa."

"Yes, and poor grandma has to listen. But my sister Lily was a much better talker. Lily and the man talked for a long time. They agreed to see each other again. They met for lunch on park benches. They went to lectures together, to the library, for long walks. They went dancing. And Lily went to a class and learned to paint. She would paint pictures for him, big pictures of nature. Oh, I could see how much she loved him. Lily didn't do so many rituals, but she started with him. She learned to bake challah. She liked that."

"What was his name?"

"His name was Saul Stiller. He was a few years younger than my sister, but remember she looked quite young. He worked in his uncle's clothing factory, but he was always reading, always studying. Every Shabbos he went to shul to pray. Every holy day he observed all the laws, but he didn't yell at anyone else if they didn't. He gave to the poor and visited the sick. A very nice man. I liked him very much.

"They planned to get married, and then came the World War. This was 1917, Lily, and the War had been going on in Europe for several years, but America was going to enter. And Saul became a soldier. I volunteered myself but they didn't take me because of my eyesight. So I wrote about the War.

"Let me tell you, plenty of Jews wanted to fight. At the end a quarter of a million Jews signed up to go over to Europe. So many of us were new to this country, and we wanted to show how grateful we were that America took us in and gave us freedom. I wrote many stories about the Jews killed and wounded in the war.

"Saul was one of those who was proud to be an American. So he went off to show America that it had been right to let in the Jews. And just before he went he asked Lily to marry him. She immediately said yes. He promised he'd be back for her. He wrote letters every day. Lily would cry over those letters. She was very scared he would get killed. There were so many deaths. But Lily forced herself to find hope. She spent many hours reading his books and studying more about painting.

"What happened to him, grandpa?"

"That's what I'm going to tell you. It happened on Yom Kippur. You know from Hebrew school that means the Day of Atonement, the day we try to make up our sins to God."

"Grandpa, maybe God can forgive me for hurting Dennis."

"I'm sorry, my little one, but on Yom Kippur you are forgiven only sins against God. If you hurt someone you have to take care of that yourself with the person you hurt if that's possible or in some other way."

"Oh. But how can I make it up to Dennis?"

"We have to think about that. First we have to see what happens to him."

"Okay, grandpa. What happened to Saul on Yom Kippur?"

"By then it was 1918. The War was drawing to an end. The Americans helped in what was called the Hundred Days Offensive. Saul was in France with the infantry.

"Now remember I said he was religious. So there it was Yom Kippur, the holiest day of the year. Saul didn't eat, even though there was going to be fighting that day and he would need the food for strength, still he didn't eat. Very early in the morning, before anyone was up, Saul got up to say the morning prayers. The only people he saw were those on sentry duty and Captain Willet, who was planning the battle. The captain came over to him and asked why he was up, and Saul explained. Then the Captain told him it was important to eat. That he'd be too exhausted to fight. The Captain invited him to breakfast with some eggs and coffee.

"But Saul, very quietly, told the Captain it was important to him to follow the customs of his people, that he would not be eating until after sundown. The Captain said he admired Saul.

"Many hours of fighting followed. Saul was indeed very tired. Finally, it was near sundown. Many enemy soldiers had been shot. Many Americans had died. You see the best of people and the worst of people on a battlefield, Lily, and Saul saw that.

"Saul was walking along when he saw an enemy who had pretended to be shot. The enemy jumped up and aimed his rifle at Captain Willett. Saul didn't hesitate for a second. He jumped right in front of the Captain and tried to push him out of the way. The Captain fell over safely, but Saul took three bullets in the stomach. The Captain shot the enemy, and then screamed out for medical help. But there was no one around because everyone was busy somewhere else. The Captain stayed with Saul, waiting for medical help to arrive.

"It took two and a half hours before any help arrived. Saul had an emergency operation, and the Captain waited outside. He prayed. He kept talking to the doctors. He volunteered to give blood or do whatever else he could."

"What happened grandpa, did Saul live?"

"When the surgery was over, that's just what the Captain asked the doctor. And the doctor said it was the strangest case he had ever seen. He said when he began he was sure that Saul would die. But the doctor said he was shocked because there was no food in Saul's stomach. If his stomach hadn't been empty, he would have died. Had he eaten on Yom Kippur, my little one, Saul would be another American soldier dead in the War.

"So you see, was it God's miracle or the doctor's or Saul's? It is a mystery."

"He was okay, grandpa?"

"It took a long time, but, yes, he was okay. He immediately wrote to Lily to tell her what happened.

"Did I ever meet Saul?"

"No, I don't think you did. He lives in Los Angeles, now. He's as old as your grandfather. If that's possible."

"Did he and Lily get married when he returned?'

"That's the saddest story in my whole life, my little one. When Lily got Saul's letter, she was so overjoyed she went out that night to eat a big meal. She said it was the happiest night of her life. On the way back from the restaurant she saw a beautiful picture in a window. She stared at it for a long time, and then she decided that for a surprise she would paint a picture in honor of Saul.

"It's the story I told you about her. It was that week-end that she went to Maine to the woods so she could paint a special picture for Saul. She worked all morning. She found a peaceful spot, because that's what she wanted for her life with Saul, just to be together in some quiet place. It's hard work to paint. She got thirsty in the woods, but she had no water. She took a drink of water from a spring flowing through the woods. Then she finished the picture.

"When she returned home, right away she got very, very sick. We called the doctor, but he couldn't help her.

"I called everyone I knew to ask if they knew how to help. But Lily didn't get better. The last time I spoke with her, she told me to write to Saul to tell him she had died but not to tell him she had been painting for him. She didn't want Saul to feel responsible. She told me to tell him that she loved him. She saw me trying to stop myself from crying, and she said I should cry because the tears would clean my soul."

My grandfather stopped speaking. I somehow knew I should not talk either.

He cleared his throat. "And after she died, I did write to Saul. But he was a smart man. I had to tell him she was painting. And he figured out by when she painted that she did it for him. Saul never married, and he never forgave himself. He asked me if he could have the painting, and, of course, I gave it to him. I spoke with him a couple of years ago, and he says he still looks at it and tries to imagine he's in that woods beside Lily."

More silence.

"That's why I'm telling you this story, my little one. There's always hope even when all looks bad like for Saul. But there's always sadness waiting around the corner, too. You have to be ready for that as well. Whatever happens, you need to seek the forgiveness of others if you can and then you need to seek the forgiveness of yourself."

I listened to my grandfather's story, and I thought there were both miracles and tragedy in life and you never knew which one you'd get. I didn't sleep very well that night, but my mother understood and let me stay up late. I did pray because I needed help beyond my own powers, beyond what I deserved.

The next day I waited to hear the results of the operation. The new school year was going to begin in a week. I knew that Yom Kippur was going to be soon after that. I asked my grandfather to take me with him to his synagogue on the Day of Atonement, and he told me he would. He told me to keep busy while I waited, so I went shopping with my mother for school supplies and new shoes.

My mother called Dennis' mother that evening. I wanted to hear and I didn't. I was afraid to find out the truth. After a minute, I saw my mother crying. My heart collapsed.

It was a few minutes later when I saw my mother run into her room.

My grandfather came to our apartment fifteen minutes later. He knocked on my door. I told him to come in.

"Lily, sit down."

I sat on the edge of my bed.

"First of all, Dennis is not dead."

I almost didn't understand the words. My heart soared like a bird at the break of morning.

"He's okay, grandpa?"

"He's not dead. But, Lily, he's not going to be the same Dennis you knew. He had some problems with his brain."

"I don't understand, grandpa."

"He'll have a hard time understanding some things.'

"Like in school."

"Dennis won't be able to go to your school anymore, Lily. It's too early, but he'll need some help your school can't give him."

"I did it, grandpa. I did it. And now I can never make it up to him."

"It was an accident, Lily. You didn't mean to do it if you even did it in the first place."

"I know, grandpa, but that doesn't help. I didn't mean to do it, but I still think I did it."

"I don't know if it will help you, Lily, but when your mama called me, I called Dennis' mama. She told me his head was at an angle when he was hit. If he had been facing the fort he would have been hit in a different place. The police say he was looking off to his side or trying to look behind him because someone called him. They don't know who it was but a couple of boys heard someone calling his name. You see, whatever happened, it was not your fault. You can't even be certain it was your rock that hit him."

"I wish I could believe all that, grandpa."

"Those are the facts, Lily. You can believe them. And now you must be tired. You get some sleep. Soon enough we can talk of atonement."

I cried myself to sleep that night.

Dennis came home eventually and he looked like a different boy. He couldn't play. When I went over to see him I couldn't bear it and ran outside. Soon, his family sent him away from the neighborhood. I tried to find out what happened to him, but I never could.

And I never learned if I had been responsible.

A few years ago I went back to Garden Bay Manor. I walked to the fort. There's a big house there now. How I wish it had been there before. I walked around the neighborhood. No one I knew remained. I walked past my old apartment, and then

I walked across the street to where Dennis had lived. I just looked up at the window. I went back to my apartment, stared at the big weeping willow, and remembered my grandfather sitting there. I went to the stores and saw that all the ones I remembered were gone.

I guess that's what happens to worlds, they are born and die just like people. One day you understand your world, and the next day it's a new world that makes no sense at all. I know when I learned about Dennis I went from living in one world to living in another.

I tried to live as normal a life as I could after Dennis. His mother was very nice to me. She had heard how I felt, and she came over with some chocolate chip cookies and told me no one blamed me and that I shouldn't blame myself. She said I shouldn't ruin my life because then there would be two tragedies.

At the end, though, I have been haunted by my grandfather's words. In the weeks that followed, my grandfather and I had many talks. I learned the obvious lesson about throwing rocks. I learned one mistake can affect you forever.

But the larger lesson for me that my grandfather taught was even more difficult, much more painful.

Every day is a Day of Atonement for me. It's not like Yom Kippur where I get atonement from God. It's my own Day of Atonement where I try to get atonement from myself. Every day I wake up, remember Dennis, and use that memory to do some good, to say a kind word, to help out someone who needs it and is too scared to ask. I've helped injured and sick children. I've volunteered, made donations, talked to grieving parents as a counselor. I've told this story to many people who needed to hear it.

But the sad truth is that I'll never know if what I've done can make up for what I did.

That, my grandfather told me, is one of the tragic mysteries of life.

CHAPTER SEVEN:
THE CUPIDS OF THE GHETTO

"When are we going, grandpa?"

"Your Aunt Ruth said to get there as quickly as possible. We'll take a train tonight."

I was excited. We would be staying with my Aunt Ruth and Uncle Sam at their beach house. I wasn't quite sure where it was other than it was near Riverhead on Long Island. Aunt Ruth was my grandfather's middle daughter, born a year after my mother.

"How long are we going to be there?"

My grandfather smiled at me. "We're invited for a few days."

"Do they really live right on the beach?"

"Just a few hundred feet from the bay's edge, my little one, so bring all your swimsuits."

"I only have one, grandpa."

"Your mother is going to Forest Hills this morning. Maybe she'll take you shopping in Alexander's, and you can buy some more."

I ran to pack. My mother did take me, and I bought two more suits, and more clothes than I expected my mother to get.

I enjoyed the train ride out to a remote place called Speonk. My Uncle Sam and my cousin Linda were waiting. Linda was a year younger than I was, but she had grown faster. I was surprised when we got off the train to see how much weight she had gained.

I could barely reach around her when we hugged.

My Uncle Sam drove us to where they lived, a place called Fannings Beach in a community called Aquebogue. I couldn't see much because it was dark when we first arrived.

Aunt Ruth was a favorite of mine. She always had a big smile, and she could cook in a way my poor mother couldn't even though she was forever trying. Linda and I ran inside. Aunt Ruth's smile was a fraction of its normal size. I wondered if she wasn't so glad to see me after all. The food tasted as though my mother had cooked it.

Uncle Sam told her what he thought of the food, and she got up and left the table. I thought my grandfather would follow her, but he didn't. Linda just looked down. Uncle Sam looked at my grandfather and said, "She's like that all the time."

My grandfather said, "Maybe she has a reason."

It was Uncle Sam's turn to get up. But he wasn't crying. He stormed outside and got into his car. The engine was loud as he drove away.

I didn't sleep well that night, wondering why my aunt and uncle were fighting like that.

The next morning, my grandfather and I went for a walk to look around.

"It's nice in the country, isn't it, Lily?"

"Yes, grandpa." I wanted to ask about what happened the night before, but I thought my grandfather would talk to me about it when he thought it was right to do so.

We walked down the dirt road to the end. There was a pump there, and my grandfather showed me how to pump water. Then we walked to the dock at the other end where some boys were fishing. I was surprised to see how many people were around, especially young people.

I couldn't hold back any longer.

"Grandpa?"

"Yes, Lily."

"I don't think Aunt Ruth wants me here."

"What makes you say that?"

"She didn't seem very happy to see me. And Uncle Sam just seemed angry."

"Aunt Ruth is just unhappy right now. And so is Sam. It doesn't have anything to do with you, Lily."

"Why are they unhappy?"

We were walking along the beach. It was still early, and there was a breeze.

My grandfather stopped walking.

"She and Uncle Sam are not getting along so well, as you could see. Uncle Sam doesn't even know why he's unhappy. I think he doesn't feel he knows his place in the world. I think he wants to go off and look to find out."

"I don't understand, grandpa."

"It's hard after you've live for a bit, Lily. You wonder if any of it makes sense. And that's got Sam very confused. He doesn't dislike you. He doesn't even dislike Ruth or Linda. He's just striking out because he doesn't know what else to do."

"What's going to happen to them, grandpa?"

"Ah, my little one, I think they're going to stop being married."

"But what about Linda? What will she do?"

"I don't know. I think she'll stay with your aunt."

"I don't know anybody who stopped their marriage, grandpa. Not anybody. Why do they need to stop?"

"Divorce never has an easy answer, my little one. Some people get married because they think the other person is pretty or handsome. But that changes, or they get so used to it they begin looking for someone else who's pretty or handsome. Some people get married because they want to escape their homes, and they end up marrying someone just like the parent they're trying to leave. Sometimes people marry because they think their spouse is their dream in life. Or they get married for practical reasons or religious reasons, or they just think that's the person they're supposed to marry."

"What should I say to Aunt Ruth, grandpa?"

"Don't say anything until she mentions it. If she does, you just say you're sorry and that you love her."

We walked for a bit, and I stopped. "Grandpa, you never told me how you met grandma and why you married her."

"So now you want to hear. I don't like to talk about it so much, Lily."

"Please, grandpa."

My grandfather looked down at me. I think he could see the hurt, the need for some kind of reassurance that the world hadn't gone off-kilter, that my own world, unlike Linda's, would stay stable.

"Okay. So you want the story. Come, let's sit on the dock."

We sat down and dangled our feet over the edge. The sun was getting warmer.

"It was a long time ago, 1924 to be precise. That's when we met. My whole world was changing then. Remember, I was a reporter for the *Forward*. But families were moving out, people didn't listen to the rabbis so much. The radio was just beginning, and in a few years it made the comedians famous. After the War, America didn't so much want the Jews to come any more. There was a big stop in immigration, so by 1924 it was almost over.

"Ah, so many were trapped in Europe, but they didn't know it. They thought America wasn't so kosher, that it was a land for unbelievers.

He paused, and his face grew very serious. "I...I have a story about before I met your grandma, but you can't say it to anyone. Not your mama or papa, or anyone in the whole world."

"Why grandpa?"

"Because it's a secret."

"A good secret or a bad secret?"

"Not such a good secret. In 1924 I was thirty-four years old. It's not like now. In those days you got married early."

"So then why did you wait, grandpa?"

"I didn't."

I was confused. "But I thought you said you met grandma when you…"

"I was engaged to someone else before I married your grandma."

My head felt light. I knew my grandfather well and deeply loved him. I thought I understood him. It was like if my mother suddenly told me I wasn't her daughter. It was like the rules of the world changed just as I was learning to play the game. I'd learn the new rules, and they'd change again. I wasn't sure I could ever keep up with the changes.

"Maybe I shouldn't say this to you, Lily. Maybe you won't think so well of your grandpa."

I think now that was exactly why he told me, to show me his own failures, to make me see him as a person not some perfect being, to let me understand that I would go through hard times and that would be all right too, that somehow I just had to put one foot in front of the other and keep walking.

"Everyone on the East Side was a matchmaker. They couldn't stand it if someone young was not married and they always had a cousin or a neighbor who was perfect for you. And it wasn't just the Jews. Some Swedish man who I met had two young daughters, blondes both of them, and pretty, and he liked me and thought I should marry one, but I told him that was not such a good idea.

"And there were professional matchmakers. We called them 'the Cupids of the Ghetto.'"

"What's a ghetto, grandpa?"

"In Europe it was a small place where they made Jews live. We weren't forced to live on the East Side, so it was partly a joke, but partly real because there were so many of us all living in the same small area, and we were all so poor at first that we were stuck there."

"I wouldn't like it if I didn't have money to buy what I needed."

"It's no fun, my little one, I can tell you that.

"Anyway, our neighbor, Mrs. Pinsky, was a shadchen, one of those matchmakers. She came to my parents and said she had a woman who was perfect for me, maybe not so religious but a gem. As sweet as the angels she said, with a voice to match. Best of all, she could play the piano beautifully. That really impressed my father. My mother wanted to know what she looked like, but the matchmaker said, "Who cares, as long as she's a good woman?' But my mother had the instincts of a bloodhound. She tracked this woman down and managed to walk by her at a pushcart where they sold peaches. My mother came home and announced her satisfaction. The woman was pretty enough."

"Weren't you angry at your parents, grandpa?"

"I didn't like it, but they just wanted the best for me. And I figured what could it hurt if I went to visit the woman? I told the matchmaker that I was making no promises.

Mrs. Pinsky told me the woman was one of five sisters, and her parents wanted her to set a model for the others who weren't yet married. No young woman wanted to be 'left,' which was the word used for the woman who didn't get married. It was a cruel word, but it was a different world."

"How much did you pay Mrs. Pinsky, grandpa?"

"The bride's family paid. They had a dowry, some money that she would bring to our marriage, and Mrs. Pinsky was going to get a percentage of it. I never learned how much, but I think it was five per cent."

"That's a strange way to get married, grandpa."

"There's no way to get married and stay married that's not strange, my little one."

I considered that, but I was way too young to grasp its wisdom.

"And Mrs. Pinsky went with me for a Shabbos dinner. I noticed that only three of the sisters were there."

"Was the other one sick?"

"They made some excuse, but I knew what it meant."

"What's that grandpa?"

"It meant the missing sister was very pretty, and I might want to marry her, so they sent her away. They wanted to push temptation out the door."

"Did you want to marry the woman you had dinner with, grandpa?"

"Sure. I thought she'd be a good wife."

"But you barely knew her."

"It was practical. Marriage then wasn't like it is today. It was an arrangement that would benefit both people. We didn't know much about love. Or I didn't. My parents wanted me to marry her. She wanted to marry. Everyone told me I should marry. And you know what, Lily? She was a good woman and I think we would have had a wonderful marriage. Love came along, I guess, whatever love is. Maybe needing each other and depending on each other. Something like that. We had that."

"Why did you say you would have had a good marriage, grandpa?"

"I'm coming to that."

"Okay. Wait, grandpa. What about the missing sister? Did you ever meet her? Was she really pretty?"

"Sure I met her. But that family wasn't crazy. They waited until after the engagement before they let me see her. And, yes, she was very pretty. But I didn't care. I was going to marry…I haven't told you her name, Lily, and I don't think I should. You shouldn't remember her too well. Is that all right?"

"What should I call her, grandpa?"

"Call her Angel."

"That wasn't her name, grandpa."

"No, it wasn't. But she became an angel, just like Mrs. Pinsky said."

"How did she become an angel, grandpa?"

"It was a few months before our planned marriage. She worked as a seamstress at a place called the Triangle Waist Company. They made blouses. She worked six days a week with Sunday off. Her pay was three dollars for the week. She was going to leave at the end of 1911 so that we could get married. She was so happy doing all the planning. Still, we needed a little money to get us going, a little more than the dowry. She was then living with her parents in a tenement on Attorney Street, and each morning she walked to work."

"Did she get hurt at work, grandpa?"

"No, not hurt. I will always remember. It was March 25, 1911. I…"

My grandfather stopped speaking. I hadn't noticed as he spoke how warm it had gotten. Now I felt the sun's heat all over me. I stared at the water below, watching the water move along. I turned and saw a motorboat in the bay. I had learned not to ask my grandfather to continue when he was silent.

Finally, his body heaved a bit. "The factory caught on fire. She was on the eighth floor. Someone who survived told me she ran to the stairway but it was crowded. My angel ran to the window, but it was no use. The fire department's ladders

LAWRENCE J. EPSTEIN

couldn't reach that high. . Hundreds of people, mostly young women, were trapped.

"I guess she decided to leap to a ladder before the fire reached her. She jumped, holding the hand of another woman. I suppose they thought they might have a chance together. But instead they died together. They landed on the ground. Two dead angels."

"I'm sorry, grandpa."

"Me, too. You can imagine so sad I was. I couldn't think about marriage again for many years. I thought I would not marry. But then I met your grandma."

"But how did you meet her, grandpa?"

Instead of answering me, he stood up. "Come, Lily, it's burning here. We have to go back. I want you to be kind to Linda, like you always are. I want to speak with Ruth. I'll tell you about grandma later."

I said okay, but I was disappointed.

When we got back to the house, my Aunt Ruth asked Linda to go outside with me. Her voice was quivering. I thought there was going to be another fight, and I was glad I wasn't going to be there. Linda looked sad and beyond my ability to help her. She and I walked to the dirt road. There was an empty lot right in front of us between two houses. We could see the water.

"I'm so scared," Linda said.

I touched her shoulder. "Maybe it's like a storm. It's bad when it's there but when it's over everything goes back to normal."

"I...Look, Lily."

I stared out at the sand in front of us. There was a single line of water working its way through the sand toward us.

"I never saw that before." She turned to me. "It's pretty. Come on, let's go see where it's coming from."

We began to walk. The line of water grew wider and deeper as we got closer to the bay. We were close to the shore, and it looked like more and more water was coming onto the sand, where it didn't belong.

It all happened so fast. One minute the water was up to our ankles, and we thought that was just nice. But then it was up to our knees, and then our waists, and it just kept rising.

Linda screamed at me, "Come on, Lily, let's go back."

We turned around and I felt water rush over my shoulders. I tripped, stood up, and screamed. It was hard to walk with the water trying to grab me and pull me down.

The water was at my throat. I turned to Linda. She was crying and struggling.

Suddenly, the arms were there. Uncle Sam picked me under one arm and Linda under the other. I didn't think he was that strong, but he held me tightly. He had to walk slowly through the water. I tried to keep my head above the water and not move. My face would get wet but then my uncle lifted me a bit and I could breathe again.

We got to a place next to Linda's house where there was dry ground. Uncle Sam put us down. He held Linda, hugged her, and cried.

"Where's grandpa?" I asked.

"He's okay," Sam said. "He's with your Aunt Ruth in another house. The flood's crested. We'll be all right now."

The woman who owned the house gave us some milk and cookies after we dried off with a towel.

It was an hour later that I saw my grandfather. I ran over to him. He bent down and I threw my arms around his shoulders.

"It's all right, Lily. Everyone's fine.'

"Uncle Sam saved us."

"I know. He was very brave. He loves you both."

I was too young to formulate the question of whether Sam had found his purpose in life in taking care of his daughter and niece. I was just grateful for what he had done.

We stayed for another day. My aunt and uncle had stopped fighting. Maybe the thought of losing Linda had scared them. At least I hoped so.

It was on the Long Island Rail Road train trip back that I asked my grandfather to tell me how he had met my grandmother.

"You're like some defense lawyer," he said, though with kindness. "You never forget and you always ask.

"All right. So I told you it was 1924. Well, that was the very first Macy's Thanksgiving Day Parade. Only then they called it the Christmas Parade. I was covering it, not for the Forward but for an English-language newspaper. The parade had started at 145th Street in Harlem, and they marched six and a half miles to the Macy's store on 34th Street near Seventh Avenue. I was standing behind a police barricade near the store.

"Your grandma Chana was working then at Macy's. Most of the marchers were people who worked there, so she was walking carrying some sign with another woman.

"Oh, you should have seen that parade, Lily. It was so crowded. One of my friends on the police told me they thought there were 10,000 people there. But of course I was very used to crowds.

"They had jugglers, a man on stilts dressed as a policeman, floats, and live animals from the Central Park Zoo. All kinds of animals, bears, donkeys, a giraffe, a gorilla, a lion, and, my favorite, a long line of elephants. Those elephants looked big, I can tell you that.

"Anyway, your grandmother was young, but she hadn't eaten that day. She was exhausted. And as I said it was a long walk. So as she got closer to the store she was more and more tired. She was about a hundred yards in front of the elephants. The way she tells it, her head became light and she wasn't so sure where she was. I could see this young woman wobbling. She walked sideward and then forward and then sideward again.

"She got to the police barricade right in front of me, and she collapsed. I jumped over, picked her up, and carried her off the street. Of course, it's possible that when I told the story to her parents the elephants may have been about to step on her instead of being a hundred yards away."

"You were her hero, grandpa."

"Some hero. She fell down in front of me. We took it as a sign. We had shared an experience together with maybe a little danger, and we fell in love."

"Does grandma still love you?"

"Most of the time, I think. Love's not such a dependable feeling for a whole life. If you just have love, it's not enough. But this wasn't an arranged marriage at least. We met each other, and we were the ones who decided to get married, not our parents. Though, I'll tell you Lily, that's not always a very dependable way to meet people to marry."

I told my grandfather the boy on television I wanted to marry.

"Oy, Lily. You should live and be happy, but don't be too surprised if he's different when he's not on tv."

I didn't understand what my grandfather was trying to say, but I let it go.

"Do you think Aunt Ruth and Uncle Sam will stay together, now grandpa?"

"What makes you ask?"

"They stopped being angry for the last day."

"Yes they did. Sam was proud of himself for saving you and Linda. Maybe that's enough for him."

"I hope so," I said.

I wish it had turned out that way. But it didn't. Aunt Ruth and Uncle Sam did get divorced about a year after our visit. Linda stayed with Ruth, but she was very unhappy whenever I saw her. She begged me to come up with a plan to get her parents back together. And, like some subject in a psychological study, Linda is now living with her third husband. I talk to her on the phone sometimes and see her at various family gatherings. Whenever I see her I am glad I'm in a happy marriage. And when I fight with my husband I remember Linda and don't fight too hard or too long.

My grandpa and grandma stayed together, of course, as did my own parents. But I'm often struck by the families my children know.

The hurt is so deep, the wound so seemingly permanent. I worry about those children.

And, alone at night after hearing another story from a friend, I wonder if those Cupids of the Ghetto were so bad after all or if freedom to choose a mate is worth all the pain it can cause. Maybe we all need a little more help than we realize and maybe the way we pick partners goes beyond the value of freedom. I wonder if too much freedom is its own jail. My grandfather used to talk about the value of self-control, but when I grew up in the 60s that kind of language was laughed at. I wonder if my grandfather knew more than my friends.

At the very bottom of night before the rosy finger of dawn appears, I understand what my grandfather taught me, that love has a test: does your life get better after you get married? If the answer is resounding yes, then despite the difficulties, you have married the right person. It is a practical and not a romantic definition of love, but I think that's what the Cupids of the Ghetto knew that we have forgotten.

And I think about the unnamed woman my grandfather almost married, and I wonder what his life would have been like. I wonder what it would have been like not to have been born.

I shake my head in the dark, and those are the nights I can't fall back to sleep.

CHAPTER EIGHT:
OUTSIDE

"Grandpa, I want to be president."

"You'll have to wait for President Eisenhower to finish his term, and, anyway, you're way too young."

"Grandpa, stop kidding. I mean president of my fifth-grade class."

"There you meet the age requirement. So what can I do to help you?"

"I need some ideas. I'm running against Neil Kenney, and everyone likes him. I'm going to make some posters this afternoon."

"Well, my little one, you could also have a little campaign rally in the neighborhood. Maybe outside Goldmark's. They let kids sell lemonade there, and it's a supermarket with a lot of customers. You could give lemonade and cookies. Or better yet if you can find someplace right near the school"

"You mean I should bribe people?"

"Of course not, Lily. I don't think your friends could be bought for a cookie. But if you wish you could sell the lemonade and cookies and talk to them about the election. The idea is to get them to come see you so you can tell them about your ideas."

"I want to do that, grandpa, but it's getting very cold outside."

"I know, but the school won't let you do it inside, and I don't think any store will either. What's Neil doing?"

"He's getting all his friends to promise to vote for him and to speak to their friends. And he's also putting signs all over the school. He's ahead of me on that."

"He's a regular Tammany Hall politician."

94

"I don't know what that is, grandpa, but he's winning I think."

"Do you have some friends who are helping you?"

"Yes, Rose Hall is a big help. She hates Neil because he always gets higher grades than she does, so she really wants me to win and show him he's not great at everything. She's been going all over the school and saying how good I am and saying how bad Neil is. I told her to talk just about me. She was upset about that because she really is helping me just to get at him. But she's doing a lot. In fact, she and her brother are coming over this afternoon to help me make the signs. I'm trying to do all I can, but I think there's a problem."

My grandfather looked at me. "What is this problem, Lily? I don't think it can be you. You're very smart, and I see that the other children like you."

I sat on the edge of the couch. I didn't know how to explain what I felt, but I thought if I tried, my grandfather might understand me.

"It's strange, grandpa. I do think people like me. They're friendly. No one makes fun of me like they do some of the other kids. But even a lot of girls told me they were voting for Neil. I wouldn't mind if they thought he'd be a better president. They even said they liked some of my ideas such as having a suggestion box and having more quizzes like spelling bees. But they said they didn't think a girl should be president."

"And how many girls told you this?"

"Two, but I think others agree with them and they're just not saying it. It's not fair, grandpa. I'm the same person as if I was a boy."

"No it isn't fair, Lily. One day maybe everything in the world will be fair, but that's a long way off. I think you'll live to see a woman president, and not of the fifth grade. Meantime, you have to be strong, but you also have to fight it. Tell your friends they're wrong. Tell them it's okay not to vote for you if they don't like your ideas but not just because you are a girl."

My grandfather sighed. "Sadly, Lily, there's always been prejudice in the world. America is a great land, and it let millions of immigrants in including Jews. But even in this great country there has been prejudice, against Indians, and the black people, and the Chinese, and the Irish, and the Italians, and lots of other people. And believe me, my little one, there was lots of prejudice against people who were Jewish."

"Did that ever happen to you, grandpa?"

"It happened to many people I know. It was really bad starting in the 1920s. But one event that I especially remembered happened in the late 1930s, in 1939 to be exact. Do you remember me telling you about Jimmy Stanton, the comedian who was in love with my sister?"

"Sure, grandpa."

"Well, Jimmy got to be a big success on radio in the 1930s. He wasn't Jack Benny, but he was very popular. The Jewish comedians were so famous on the radio because their humor was in their talking. There weren't so many Jews who were funny in silent pictures. But in radio they were big. And Jimmy was among them. He had his own show. I used to visit him while he was on the air because the shows were funny and interesting to watch, especially how they did the sound effects. Also, he introduced me to famous people, and I could write stories about them.

"In the late 1930s anti-Semitism was especially bad because Hitler had come to power in Germany and lots of people here didn't want to believe what was happening to the Jews there. Of course we had no idea about how bad it could get. We didn't have a lot of power to convince the American people that the Jews were in trouble. A lot of people, not everyone, probably not even the majority of Americans, but a lot of people thought

Jews were behind Communism in Russia and that Jews had caused the Depression. I know what they said from my work as a reporter. People would say Jews were greedy or dishonest or that they controlled the banking system, which, believe me Lily, was so ridiculous that I sometimes laughed at people when they said it. I couldn't help myself.

"I had by then left the *Forward* and was working completely for an English language paper in New York. They didn't want me to cover these stories so much. And I fought with them, but they didn't print the stories I wrote. Finally, they told me if I handed in another story about prejudice against Jews I'd get fired.

"Now there was a big World's Fair in 1939. Everyone was there. They opened it on April 30th because that was the anniversary of George Washington taking the oath of office as America's first president. He took that oath in New York City. I was very excited. That story they liked. I just stood there and interviewed people. It was a natural.

"But I have to tell you about one bad incident in particular that took place at the World's Fair, and it starts with a bad person. His name was Father Coughlin. Everyone was very careful about what they said about him because he was a priest. Now I was friends with priests, and all the ones I knew were wonderful, very kind, very understanding. But this Father Coughlin he was a bad one.

"Too many Americans listened to his radio show. When he was most popular forty million people listened each week. They listened to his hatred. He became a hero in Nazi Germany. He kept attacking Jews. People were afraid to stand up to him.

"One guy who did stand up was a comedian friend of Jimmy's. His name was Eddie Cantor. Back then he was very famous and had a big radio show himself. Anyway, at the World's Fair, Eddie held up a picture of a check given by a pro-

Nazi group to Father Coughlin and said Coughlin was 'playing footsie with the Nazis.'

"I was there and I interviewed Eddie right after. Let me tell you, Lily, he was one brave man. I didn't realize how brave until the next day when his sponsor, a cigarette company, cancelled his radio broadcast. Although he was very famous, he was not allowed back on radio for over a year.

"Meanwhile, I had to decide what to do with my story. I had this great story, but my editor didn't want any more stories about hatred of the Jews. And he didn't want to offend readers who liked Father Coughlin. But I wanted to give him the story knowing that it might cost me my job. Well, finally, I..."

There was a loud knock at my door. I ran to get it, and it was Rose and her brother. I ran back to my grandfather.

"Grandpa, can you finish the story later? Rose is here."

"Of course, my little one. You go get elected president."

We went into my room. Rose closed the door. Then she turned and began to cry.

"What's the matter?"

Rose's brother spoke up: "She did something real bad. So bad she couldn't tell our mother."

"I didn't mean to." Rose was loud.

"All right," I said, "Tell me what happened."

Rose nodded, but it was a minute before she could speak. "I was so mad at Neil and every time I saw one of his signs at school I got madder and madder. I tried taking them off, only they wouldn't budge. So I got an idea. I figured it would be fun to take a little paint and paint over his face. Then everyone would laugh at him, and they wouldn't vote for him any more.

"Well, my daddy had some paint in the basement of our building, so I took a couple of small cans, something to open the cans, and a brush and hid them in my school bag. I knew how to open the paint cans because I had helped my daddy paint a bookcase for someone. Anyway, I took them with me and waited until after school. Instead of walking home, I went around the school painting those posters."

"That wasn't very nice," I said, "But it doesn't sound as bad as I thought it was going to be."

"She's not done," her brother said.

"Oh."

Rose looked up at me. "I wasn't as good a painter as I thought. I didn't realize that the paint would drip and go all over the place, and I didn't see at first because I'd do one poster quickly and rush to another poster. By the time I realized what happened I had already painted on ten of them."

"Well, what happened?"

"The paint got all over the school walls. I don't know if anyone saw me, but they'll know it was someone who wants you to win, and everybody knows that's me. If my parents find out, they'll kill me."

"She gets into lots of trouble," her brother said, "She's sure to get spanked bad for this one."

"And I don't have any money to pay the school. My father sure won't pay. Maybe they'll make me stay and clean it up, only I don't know how to do that."

I thought for a minute. "I don't have the money, either."

"What are we going to do?" Rose asked.

I sat on the floor and thought. "I don't know."

"My parents are gonna kill her," her brother said.

"Is your mother here?" Rose was hopeful that someone could save her.

I shook my head. "Only my grandpa. But he's pretty smart. He gets lots of good ideas. I think we should ask him."

Rose shook her head. "I don't know. I don't want to get into trouble. Maybe he'd tell my parents."

"No, my grandpa can keep a secret, and he's good at figuring out how to get out of trouble."

"Okay, I guess if we have to." She sighed.

I went out of the room. My grandfather was reading a book.

"Grandpa, Rose is in trouble. And maybe I am, too."

He quickly put the book down. "So what is this trouble, my little one?"

I told him the story.

"This Rose wasn't thinking so much with her head, was she?"

"Maybe not, grandpa, but it's too late to think what she should have done. She's already in trouble. And maybe I am, too, because everyone will think I did it or thought of it."

My grandfather went with me into my room. He sat on the chair and Rose, her brother, and I sat on the floor in front of him.

"I'm not going to spend the time telling you this was not so good, Rose. We have to figure out what to do. I have an idea."

I looked at Rose and nodded. "What's that, grandpa?"

"First, I think I should call the school and tell them what happened. Then we have to come up with a way to fix it. All right?"

"Do we have to tell them?" Rose asked.

"Don't you think it's better if we tell them than if they find out?"

"I guess so."

"Good. Then is everyone agreed?"

We all nodded now.

My grandfather left us alone while he went to make the call. All of us were quiet, looking down.

He came back in about fifteen minutes. "Okay. The principal was still there. She had to stay because of the mess. She was very angry because she likes a clean school. I explained that it was a mistake. She said it would cost fifty dollars to fix it all up. They can do it, in fact they're doing it now, and I said all of you would pay the repair costs."

"But I can't pay," Rose wailed, "And I can't ask my parents."

"They'll kill her," her brother added.

"And I don't have any money, grandpa. What should we do?"

My grandfather thought for a few minutes. "You have to sell lemonade and cookies until you make the money. And you'd better do it tomorrow right after school."

"But it's too cold then."

"Then sell hot chocolate and cookies. Rose, you can tell your mama it's for the school, which is true."

"We can do that," I said. "Mama will make lots of hot chocolate and buy lots of cookies if I tell her it's for the school."

The next afternoon was even colder than I expected. The wind whipped at my face and went right through me. My grandfather and Rose's brother walked back and forth to my apartment getting new cookies and chocolate while Rose and I stood in front of Goldmark's and sold the stuff. Lots of people went to shop in the big market, and quite a few stopped to ask what we were selling and how much it cost..

As it got darker, the cold increased. I was shaking.

"I can't keep going," Rose said. "I'm too cold. I want to go inside where it's warm."

"Grandpa, we're shaking. We've got to stop."

"No, Lily. You can't stop. You're close, but you don't have enough money. You have to stay here until you do."

I was sad and frozen. I don't ever remember being so cold. I felt a wave of sympathy for people who didn't have a warm place to go. Grandpa went back to the apartment to get more chocolate, and we kept going.

It was getting really dark. There were fewer customers.

Then, suddenly, a man approached. I recognized him as one of my grandfather's friends.

"What's this?" he asked.

"We're selling cookies and hot chocolate for our school," I said.

"Ah, I love school. I had to leave. How I wish I could have stayed like you. I'll tell you what. I'll buy all your cookies and hot chocolate."

I was excited. We gave it all to him, and he gave us the money, but we were still $5.50 short of what we needed.

"Why do you girls have such long faces?" the friend asked.

"We need to raise five and a half dollars more."

He reached into his wallet and took out a ten dollar bill. "You didn't think I wasn't going to tip you for your good service, did you?"

My eyes widened when I saw the money.

"Thank you!"

Rose and I each ran to our own home.

I told my grandfather we were done, that we had enough money. He said he would pay the school the next day and all would be settled. Then I told him about his friend, and he seemed pleased.

After dinner that night, I went over to my grandfather's apartment to thank him again and to ask him to finish his story about the priest on the radio.

He settled down in his chair, put his feet up, and said to me, "So there I was with an interview with Eddie Cantor, one of the most famous comedians in America. No one else had it, only it wasn't a story about comedy but about the Nazis and American anti-Semitism.

"I made my decision to take a chance, so I went to my editor and showed it to him. He told me it was a good story, well-written, hard-hitting, words he didn't always use about my writing. Then he said he couldn't use it. And he asked me if I remembered the warning that I'd be fired if I handed in another of those stories. I told him I did remember, but this was a huge story and we were missing it. He said it was his job to decide what stories we were missing, that too many of the Jewish leaders thought anything that happened to them should be what was in the news. I stopped him and told him that was wrong. That the Nazis were different. He said Americans didn't want to go to Europe to fight another war, that what was happening over there was their headache and not ours. He asked me if I liked my job. I told him I did. He asked me if I was going to forget the stories about supposed anti-Semitism and give him stories his readers wanted. Because, he said, if I didn't want to do that I should quit right then and there."

"What did you do, grandpa?"

"Ah, my little one, it was not a difficult choice. Whenever I have to choose between doing what I think is right and not doing it, the choice is made very easy. I told him that I couldn't keep working for him. He reminded me that the Depression wasn't finished, that I'd have a hard time getting a job. I told him I'd sweep the floors before I'd stop writing about what was happening to the Jews."

"Did you get another job?"

My grandfather shook his head. "Not right away. It was very difficult. Experience is a good teacher, but it can be a costly one. I did odd jobs, worked in some factories, wrote freelance for where I could. It was only when war came that I got a job again as a reporter. Suddenly everyone was a patriot and the Nazis were evil. Of course, no one knew just how evil until after the war."

He stopped and stared off into space. "But I can't forgive myself."

"What do you mean, grandpa?"

"I mean in a small way it was difficult for your grandma and the children. But in a much bigger way, I failed to tell the story of the Nazi danger. I should have made a bigger noise. That's the worst part. It's difficult to live with."

"But even you didn't know, grandpa."

"No, but I was a reporter. I should have figured a way to find out more. There's no sadness like the knowledge that I might have been better.

"Ah, my little one. Anyway, so you made your money. And the election will take place. And the world will go on however your grandpa feels.

"I think we deserve some hot chocolate, ourselves. Don't you?"

"I sure do, grandpa."

I know this makes me sound dense, but it took me many years before I realized that my grandfather had given his friend the money to buy the cookies and hot chocolate from us. I asked my grandfather about it, and he said he thought I had suffered enough. Then he told me I really hadn't deserved to be told to stand there in the cold, that it had been Rose's fault. He told me that sometimes we're responsible for more than ourselves, that we have to help our friends in trouble, and that going through difficult moments helps us relieve any guilt we might have.

I wasn't sure about all that, but I knew that after my grandfather paid back the school, I felt much better. Rose's parents never found out, or didn't say so if they had.

I lost the election for president of the fifth grade. Neil trounced me, in fact. But he said nice words about me and asked that I be the vice-president because he liked some of my ideas. And in front of everyone he said a girl could be just as good a president as a boy. I was proud of him. And I was proud of myself the next year because I did become president of my sixth grade class.

But most of all, I learned what it was like to be outside, to suffer unfairly, to be a loser, to be considered not good enough because I was a girl.

I also learned from my grandfather that not everyone who is outside deserves sympathy, and not everyone who is inside deserves scorn. It's the unfair prejudice that carries the real sting. So every time I feel the cold now, I am reminded that there are people who remain outside and don't deserve to be there.

I try to figure out how to open the doors that I can to let them inside.

CHAPTER NINE:
THE DEAD

"Grandpa, what happened to the Jews during the war?"

"Why do you ask, Lily?"

"We have to write a Special Interest report for our sixth grade class, and Mrs. Reynolds told me I should read Anne Frank's diary and write about the Jews."

"It's a very sad book, but a very important one."

"I know, but I want to find out what happened to her after she was captured from the attic. I want to know what life was like for the Jews. I asked mama, and she said it was not good to talk about such matters, that I should pick another Special Interest subject. And I tried to find material in the library, but there wasn't too much. And then I sat down to write with what I had, and I couldn't do it. You always told me I had to care about what I wrote, and feel it. I felt it from reading the Diary, but I didn't have enough to write about."

"Did you tell your mama that you were going to ask me?"

"No, grandpa. I thought she'd tell me that I shouldn't."

"I wasn't there. I read the papers, but they didn't say too much. We saw the newsreels afterwards of the dead bodies and the living who were almost dead."

"Do you think I should pick another subject?"

My grandfather sipped from his tea. "It's a very painful story for someone your age, Lily."

"But Anne Frank was just a little older than I am, and she had to live through it. I just want to learn about it. I know it was terrible, but I want to know."

My grandfather lowered his head. "That's a lot of evil to wade through for anyone who's genuinely human. It's easier to look away not just because of the pain it causes, but because the truth of what happened can change people. Your mama is afraid learning about it will scare you and harm you. She's afraid it will frighten you to be Jewish or even make you feel ashamed or hide your religion from others. Sometimes people who learn about evil get scared to live or think life is without meaning or, in some cases though this would never happen to you, they become attracted to the evil and become worse themselves."

"I thought you would understand, grandpa. I can't be afraid to look just because it's scary or might affect me, can I? Otherwise I'd never look at what I don't already know."

"You'd make a good journalist, Lily, always going after the story. The hardest lesson in life is that you have to recognize evil, and face it, and fight it all without becoming evil yourself. You have to be mean to the mean without becoming mean to the nice or changing yourself inside. And it's hard to face someone evil. It's hard to hurt another person. It's easy when they shoot someone on television, but in real life when you face evil all you see is another human being. It's not so easy to shoot.

"I don't think you can find what you want in books, Lily, and I don't have the film to show you. But I do have an idea."

"What's that, grandpa?"

"A dozen years ago, right after the war in 1946, the very year in which you were born, the son of a distant cousin of mine, once removed here or there, had been in a concentration camp before he came to America. He was nineteen years old then and stayed with your grandma and me. Of course your mama was married and pregnant with you. This was just before you were born, so she didn't see too much of my cousin. And she didn't like him when she did see him. He was not easy to live with then, and your grandma and I didn't know if we could let him continue to stay with us. He screamed in the night. He hid food in his room. He played a game with me, saying he could hide in his room without me finding him. He wouldn't allow sunlight into our apartment. He stared at our neighbors, and they became frightened of him. He slept in his clothes, even his shoes. His eyes were wild. He got angry easily and cursed at people. We couldn't take it.

"And then one day, several weeks after he came here, he told me a story about himself. And after that I understood him more. It was not that he became easy. I just understood. I learned to be patient. We have talked through the years, and he told me more stories. He's better now, calmer. He still has nightmares but in the day he's good. If you want to learn about what happened to the Jews, Lily, I think you should talk to my cousin Yaakov, Jacob to the public but Yaakov in the family. He's in the diamond business and lives in the city.

"But, Lily, I'm not sure if I should just take you. I think you need to ask your mama's permission."

"She might say I can't see Yaakov."

"She's my daughter and your mama. I have to consider her feelings and so do you. She deserves to be a mama."

"All right."

I trudged over to my apartment. My mother was cooking dinner.

"Mama, I have a question."

"What's that, Lily? And do you want to help me? You can make the potatoes."

I hated to cook, but I said I would help.

"Mama, I want to meet one of your relatives, grandpa's cousin."

"It's good to be interested in family. Someday we'll make a big family tree, and you'll see how many relatives you have."

"So can I go, mama?"

"I guess so. I...Lily, are you talking about that man who lived with my parents after the war?"

"Yes, mama."

"Why would you ever want to meet him? I remember him. He was horrible. Very dirty. I stayed away from him because I thought he was so dirty he would make me sick and through me make you sick."

"He's changed, mama. He's clean now. And you know I like to collect stories."

"Just like your grandfather. Yes, I know. His stories won't help you, Lily. He had a horrible life over there. I wouldn't dare listen to him. I don't know what he did in Poland, and I don't want to know. I would think you have friends to laugh with and games to play without having to listen to terrible stories."

"Maybe it will make me appreciate my life here more, mama, if I hear how bad his life was when he was my age."

My mother laughed. "You are a sly devil, Lily. I can tell what you're doing. Still there is a Yiddish proverb that 'If you can't be grateful for what you have, then at least be thankful for what you have been spared.' You tell grandpa you can talk to this man about his childhood, but I don't want you talking about when he was in some camp or to hear any stories about the Nazis. That will just upset you."

"I won't ask him to tell me those stories mama, but I can't control what he says."

"Oy. A lawyer. Your mind has all the twists of a maze, Lily. All right, you go with your grandpa. And tell him to stop the man if the talk gets bad. And don't you ask any questions about the camp. Do you promise?"

"I promise, mama."

So on the following Sunday, my grandfather and I got a ride from my father to the subway station and rode into Manhattan. When we were there, we took another subway, got out. I was lost, but my grandfather knew just where he was going.

We ended up near Second Avenue. We walked into the building and over to the elevator. It was small, and it creaked. I was scared as we rode up to the right floor. When we stepped out of the elevator, it was dark in the hallway, and there was a musty smell. Suddenly, I felt very scared and reached over to hold my grandfather's hand. We found the apartment, and my grandfather rang the bell.

It took a minute but finally someone opened the door. He was stooped over, but he had a nice smile. His head was large and round. His skin was pinkish, and he had almost no hair. He and my grandfather hugged. Then my grandfather introduced me. Yaakov peered over his gold-framed glasses at me. He had a kind face.

"So you're the famous, Lily. Come, my wife made some cake before she went out."

We walked over to the table, and there were three plates waiting and tea for him and my grandfather. We sat down. I ate the cake while Yaakov and my grandfather talked. Finally, Yaakov turned to me.

"Tell me Lily, how are you doing in school?"

I told him about my teacher and some of the students. He leaned forward to listen carefully. When I had finished, I turned to why I was here. "And I wanted to write my Special Interest report about Jews in the war, but nobody will talk to me about it. Nobody will tell me. They think I'm too young."

"They are afraid of the truth, Lily. I think humans should hear the truth, the worst of what other humans can do. But not everyone agrees, and my own story is very sad."

"I know."

"You're sure you want to hear it?"

"Yes, but I have a problem."

"What's that?"

"I promised my mama I can't ask you questions about the camp, only about your childhood."

"And you want to know what your mama does not want me to tell you?

"Yes."

"So, don't ask me questions. I'll just talk." He turned to look at my grandfather who gave him a short, sharp nod.

He took a sip of his tea while I ate some more cake. "We lived in Gorlice, by the Carpathian Mountains, south of Krakow. You know Polish geography?"

I shook my head.

He got up, found a map, and pointed out Gorlice on the map.

"The Nazis came right away, just a few days after they invaded Poland. This was in September 1939. I was very young, but I was big and I was strong. They told us that people my age had to show up every day at the magistrate's office so we could work. They waited until the evening of Yom Kippur and tore apart the inside of the synagogue to make it into a stable. They killed any Jews they found praying. I lived like this for several years until 1942 when they sent me to Belzec, a camp. They put us in a cattle car, a couple of hundred of us without food or water. We stood there for a day. Many tried to escape, to break through the floor or the walls. The guards kept shooting."

"Did you try to escape?" I asked.

Yaakov looked down. "I could not. I had to protect my younger sister." The words came out in a whisper.

He cleared his throat and continued. "When we got there, they separated men from women. I saw some soldiers drag off my sister. I didn't find out what happened to her until later. They shaved her head, and she walked into the death chamber."

"She was killed?" I asked.

He stared at me. "She was your age."

"Yaakov," my grandfather said, but he said it gently.

Yaakov turned to him. "She wants to know. It's better to live by illusions in life?"

My grandfather said, "Some people have a deep need for illusions, Yaakov. And most of the rest of us need some. It hurts too much not to do so. You're not doing her any favors telling her not to have any illusions."

"I learned to live without them."

"And is that how you want her to live?"

Yaakov looked down at the floor. His face became determined and he raised his head and looked at me. "I was strong then, young. They gave me a job."

"Yaakov!" My grandfather's voice was stronger.

Yaakov ignored him. "I had to recover the dead bodies."

My grandfather looked at me. I hadn't flinched. My grandfather saw that I was listening. I stared directly into Yaakov's eyes as he continued speaking. "They used diesel engines to pump in carbon monoxide gas to one of the extermination cells. There were four of them. Sometimes the diesel engines broke down and the Jews had to wait in the death chamber. People told me some prayed. Some screamed. Many must have cried. They were crowded together.

"It was my job to get them after they were killed. They had no place to fall so they were dead but they looked like they were standing up."

"Enough, Yaakov," my grandfather said.

"Do you want to hear more?" Yaakov asked me.

I nodded.

"Let her hear. You don't see young people like this. Let her hear."

My grandfather didn't speak, so Yaakov continued, "I could tell who belonged together because they were holding each other's hands. My job was to take them out and bury the bodies. Some people looked for the gold in their teeth. I did not have to do that. I dragged the dead Jews to large pits and threw the bodies down into the pit.

"I survived all this. I survived the animals in the beds and food, the screaming in the night, watching my friends die each day, the thousand pains we felt every single second.

"It was on a cold, cloudy night that a Nazi soldier took me with him into a nearby field. He had seen me around and knew me. I thought he was going to shoot me just for fun. They did that, line up Jews to see how many heads a single bullet could pass through. He took me there to the middle of the field and stopped. I was shivering in the dark. There was no one around to see him shoot me. But instead of raising his weapon he handed me a card with his name on it. He told me he was letting me go, but that in return I had to tell people after the war that he had saved my life. He was trying to protect himself in case he was ever captured, to have a witness to his kindness. He had killed who knows how many, and I was to be the proof of his humanity. He had a backpack on, took it off, and handed me a new pair of shoes and a little food and water. I fled.

"I slept in barns or under trees. I kept walking, not sure where I was going, looking for the Americans. I traveled only in the dark. I stole food and clothing when I could."

Yaakov was silent for a few seconds. "There is more I did to stay alive. But the important point is that I lived, and I did find the Americans. And then I came here and your grandfather and grandmother took me in. I was a mess. Your grandfather was the very soul of kindness to put up with me. I was a wild animal, not used to living like a human being, not used to help from other people. I had to learn again, like a little child. But your grandfather taught me. My body had been spared, and your grandfather found my hidden sanity. He brought me back to life."

LAWRENCE J. EPSTEIN

Yaakov sipped his tea again. "Slowly, I started becoming human again, and my eyes were shocked at what I saw. Here were all these people who had not gone through what I had, but they hadn't learned how to live. I saw them walking around, from their job to their house to a restaurant, to a theater, to a bar, to a store, to a thousand places, and they didn't know what they were doing or why they were doing it. I had seen the dead, Lily, and in New York I saw people who didn't know they were alive, who didn't appreciate what being alive even meant. They talked and laughed, but they were dead inside. Only their outside was alive.

"Believe me. I'm an expert on the dead, and they were dead. I yelled at them in the streets, asked them if they ever cried and dropped to the ground to look at the miracle of a blade of grass. I asked them if they ever bent over a flower and whispered to it. I cried to them that they needed more than a new car, a big house, or someone new to kiss. Of course, everyone thought I was crazy. But I was sane. They were crazy because they did not even know they were dead inside."

My grandfather put his hand on Yaakov's arm. Yaakov calmed down and nodded.

"And so I lived on my own, carrying the pain of the past and the new pain of seeing these people."

"What happened to the Nazi?" I asked.

"After the war, I did not know how to find out. But my boss had friends to call, someone in the Army I think. The Nazi died. Killed by the great American soldiers."

"What would you have done if he had lived? Would you have said he saved you?"

Yaakov looked at me. "I would have told the truth. But I would not have stopped with my story. I would have said he let me go, but he sent thousands of others to the pit. I was ready to

114

speak for the dead, to be a witness for them in the land of the living."

"How did you get better?"

He shrugged. "What was there to do except get better? Surrender? Give the Nazis another Jew? No I had to get better. I got a job. I got married."

"Please, Yaakov. Careful." My grandfather's voice was as sad as I had ever heard it.

Yaakov stared at me. His eyes were wilder. "Do you want to hear about my wife?"

"That's not fair, Yaakov," my grandfather said. "Of course she wants to hear."

Yaakov just stared at him.

My grandfather gave a sigh of resignation. He had brought me, and now he and I would both have to listen.

Yaakov bent over and stared directly into my face. "After a few years here, I met a very nice, very refined young woman. She was living with her parents. Her mother worked with the diamonds like I did, and she told me about the daughter. So I went there on a Friday night for dinner. The woman was quiet. Her eyes darted all over. I recognized that.

"Her father told me they had all been in the camps. Anyway, I thought the young woman was very pretty. Her being quiet did not bother me, even though I am a talker myself. Soon, I considered marriage, but she told me she could not marry me, that she had seen me to please her parents, but she could never marry."

He looked at my grandfather. "Remind me, Benjamin, you told me some American expression."

"I told you she was the girl of your dreams but for her all men were her nightmare."

"A nightmare, yes. She could not dream of marrying. She kept a secret locked up as tightly as I had locked up my hope.

So I came to her one day and said to her I would understand if it was just me she didn't want to marry, but I couldn't understand why she didn't want to marry anyone. I begged her to tell me why she couldn't marry, that I would understand, and that I would still want to marry her whatever the reason and however she felt.

"She sat still for a long time. Then she said she would tell me a story and then I would not want to marry her. She told me a long story about being in a camp, and about how they did experiments on her."

"What kind of experiments?" I asked.

Yaakov looked at my grandfather. Their eyes reached an understanding and Yaakov turned back to me.

"That I dare not say. For this no one is old enough. But after the experiments she could not have a baby. She was doomed to live out her life alone. I cried when I heard the story, and I told her I loved her and wanted to be her husband forever. That we would be a family, just the two of us.

I looked around as he said it and realized there were no toys, no signs of children. I don't know why, but I suddenly felt overwhelmed by a sadness I had never felt before.

Yaakov cleared his throat. "We got married, and we went to doctors. To many of them. But they all told us the same. We could not have children. Every day the silence of the children we do not have overwhelms me like a wave. When I die, all my memories will die with me."

"No, they won't," I said. "You've told them to me, and I'll remember them."

Yaakov patted me on the top of my head and turned to my grandfather. "Tell me Benjamin what did you do to deserve such a wonderful granddaughter?"

My grandfather smiled.

Yaakov turned back to me. "It is the words of the children that make me happy. Thank you, Lily."

I smiled.

Yaakov wrapped up some of the cake for me, and my grandfather and I took the subway back to Queens. We didn't talk on that trip. My grandfather let me absorb the story I had heard. Even then, I knew I would never truly be able to understand what happened.

I tried to think of what Anne Frank went through, to see what she saw as she died, to feel those feelings of a life ending.

My parents had gone to visit my aunt, so when I got home, I ran to my room and began writing. I wrote all I could remember and added it to the notes I had gotten from the books in the library. The words cascaded out of me so powerfully that I could not have stopped writing if I had wanted to do so. I pictured what was happening. The words took me over.

I was exhausted when I finished writing. I suddenly didn't feel like a sixth-grade student, but like a journalist, the way my grandfather had been.

My parents came back about seven o'clock. I had finished writing and was reading a book.

My mother asked me about the trip, and I just told her Yaakov had been very kind. She saw that I wasn't crying or scared, so she didn't ask me any more questions. Instead, she said she was going to prepare supper. My father sat down to read a newspaper.

I stood in the doorway for a long while and watched my mother. And while I stared at her, very slowly, very painfully, my mind gave birth to a thought, and the thought kept growing until I could see it plainly.

As I stood there, I wondered if my mother was dead inside. And I wondered if I would be when I grew up.

CHAPTER TEN:
THE TREASURE HUNT

"Grandpa, do you have a candle?"

My grandfather was sitting at his typewriter writing. He stopped, turned to me, and said, "Sure. In the kitchen." I suddenly realized I had interrupted him, but he didn't seem upset.

"Come," he said, "I'll show you."

We started walking, and he asked me, "Why do you need a candle, Lily?"

"For a treasure hunt. It's a contest at P.S. 2. Anyone in the sixth grade can compete."

We had reached the kitchen, and my grandfather searched until he found a candle.

"So what else are you looking for?"

"I don't know, grandpa. I have to solve the riddles."

"What do you mean?"

"We all got some riddles. The answers to the riddles were what we had to get. And there's a last riddle which we just have to answer. The candle was for one of the riddles."

My grandfather looked at my paper.

"I see. So the riddle is: 'If I put it out, its life becomes longer.' Yes, that's a candle. How did you figure it out?"

I looked down. "I didn't think mama would know, but papa did know, only he was too busy to get the candle."

"And you're allowed to ask adults?"

"Oh, yes. They said that."

"Okay, then. What's your next riddle? I didn't go to a nice school like yours. This is my chance."

"You wouldn't fit at the desks grandpa."

"Maybe a little too much cheesecake now and then. So tell me."

I looked down. "What has feet but cannot walk?"

"You know this one, Lily?"

"I'm not sure. I was thinking of an animal after an accident, but I don't think they'd put that in a quiz for school."

"Ach. You watch too much television. No gruesome stuff. There's enough outside. I know the answer."

"You do, grandpa?"

"Sure, it's a yardstick. It has three feet."

"I should have gotten that, grandpa."

"See how good I could be if I was in sixth grade now. But I don't have a yardstick. We'll have to go to a store. You have any more riddles?"

"I got most of them. Like it said 'What has hands but doesn't feel anything?' and I knew that was a clock. But I'm stuck on part of another one. The question is 'What's black when you get it, red when you use it, and white when you're done with it?' I can't get it."

"You remember going to your uncle and aunt's house last summer, and they cooked hot dogs and hamburgers out in the back yard on a grill?"

"I remember grandpa."

"They used charcoal. Think about a piece of charcoal. First it's black, and then when it burns it's red, and when it's finished burning it's a piece of white ash."

"You're smart grandpa."

"I don't know how smart it is to remember a piece of charcoal, but I'll take any compliment, Lily. So we need a yardstick and a piece of charcoal. Let's take a walk."

We went outside. The air was fresh and clean. I enjoyed walking with my grandfather. Just as we began, I asked, "Did you ever go on a treasure hunt, grandpa?"

He thought for a minute, "Not like this one. But of another kind, yes."

"Tell me about it."

"It was ten years ago, in 1948. You were a young one, almost two years old. I had a job as a reporter for a big Jewish newspaper. As it turned out, they sent me to the Middle East and by accident it was the perfect moment, for while I was there, Israel declared its independence on May 14th. I wrote about that, but it's what happened the day before that was sort of like a treasure hunt."

"What did you search for?"

"I have to tell you the background. While I was there, I did a lot of interviews. That's what we did as reporters. Talk to everyone we could, get every side. So on the day before, I was talking with a man named Otto Wallisch. He was an artist who had been born in Czechoslovakia. I was writing a story about him because he had designed Israel's first postage stamp. Now that was a story, but it was strange because the name of the country wasn't on the stamp. They were still debating whether to name it Israel or Zion or Judea or some other name."

"What did he do for the stamp, grandpa?"

"Otto wrote 'Doar Ivre,' which means Hebrew Mail. Anyway, while I was there interviewing Otto, another man burst inside. His name was Ze'ev and he was in charge of making arrangements for the Independence Day announcement. Otto introduced me, and Ze'ev said that David Ben-Gurion, the head of the people in Israel, was going to announce independence the very next day at four p.m. in the Tel Aviv Museum. Now May 14th was a Friday, so all had to be done before the Sabbath began at sundown.

"Ze'ev put Otto in charge of getting some of what they needed for the ceremony. Ze'ev gave Otto money. It was about $450 in U.S. money only it was in British pounds. Otto asked me to help. That was sort of a treasure hunt."

"What were you looking for, grandpa?"

Before my grandfather could answer, we had reached the store, the one where I had replaced the candy. Grandpa found a yardstick. We bought it from Mr. Kleinman, and he and my grandfather spoke for a moment. We still needed a piece of charcoal, so we went next door to Goldmark's. They sold charcoal, but not by the piece. My grandfather told our dilemma to someone, and he walked away for a minute and came back with a piece of charcoal. "It fell out of the bag," he said.

"Lucky for us," my grandfather said.

"And next time let me win."

My grandfather played cards once a week, and this man must have been in the game.

"For a piece of coal?' my grandfather asked.

The man shrugged.

We walked outside.

"And now, Lily, do you have all you need?

"Yes, grandpa. Except for the last question, which I just have to figure out."

"What is it?"

I looked down and read it aloud, "I precede the start of a ballgame. I am three steps away from the head of a giraffe and three steps away from the start of this riddle? Who am I?"

My grandfather took a look at the puzzle. "This is for sixth graders?"

"I guess so."

"Now I can see why I'm not in sixth grade. Let me think about this."

"Okay, grandpa, but tell me about your treasure hunt. You didn't say what you were looking for."

"All right. But first let's have an ice cream soda. We went to the luncheonette on the corner, sat down, and ordered. Mr. Belzer brought the sodas. He still looked sad, like he was always about to cry.

My grandfather turned to me and said, "Have you ever heard of Theodor Herzl?"

"No, grandpa."

"He was the man who got people excited about returning to the land and who organized the Zionist Congress."

"Was he there?"

"No, Lily. He died long ago. He was only forty-four years old when he died. Such a shame, but he died to build his dream. Anyway, Otto was supposed to get a big portrait of Herzl to place above the stage. We went all over, and finally to a place devoted to Jewish history. There, in the basement, was the portrait we needed. Only it was covered in dust. That was our first treasure on the hunt.

"We cleaned off the portrait and hauled it away. Then we had to get two big flags to hang on either side of the portrait. The problem was they had to be very big. Oy, it was hard to find those flags. We did, but they were filthy with dust, and we couldn't clean them off."

"What did you do, grandpa?"

"What did we do? What do you do with dirty cloth? We took the two flags to a laundry, and we cleaned them there."

"Were there any other treasures you had to look for?"

"Some others, but the hardest was to come. We had to find parchment on which the Declaration of Independence could be written. Otto was so particular. We looked here. We looked there. Each parchment he saw he didn't like. He got angry at me when I said to just pick one. He said this was for the Declaration of Independence of the Jewish people who had returned to their land after two thousand years. The parchment had to last another two thousand years at least. So we kept looking. Finally, he found one that he liked. We took it to an engineering institute to have it chemically tested, but the place was closing, so they asked Otto why he needed it in such a hurry. But, Lily, he couldn't tell them. And so they refused to do it."

"Did Otto go somewhere else to have it tested?"

"What Otto did was drag me to his home, and we stayed up all night testing the parchment to make sure it was good enough. And it was."

"That was some treasure hunt, grandpa. But did you attend the ceremony?"

"I sure did. It was very exciting, but that's for another time."

I was disappointed because I wanted to hear the story. We finished our ice cream sodas. My grandfather said good-bye to Mr. Belzer who silently waved at us. Then we started to walk home.

"Grandpa, have you had a chance to think about the last riddle?"

"I had a chance to think about who we should ask? You know Mr. Goldberg from around the corner?"

I shook my head.

"A very smart man. He studied to be a rabbi, and then he left his studies. Everyone else worked and Goldberg read books. I once saw him reading while he walked on the streets. His father was in the toy business, made a lot, let his son be a scholar. That's not always so good."

"Why grandpa?"

"It takes you away from life. Books and life. You need a balance. Some people only live and never study. That's no good either. So I took Goldberg around, showed him some life."

"That was nice of you."

"You think life is so pretty to look at, Lily? Goldberg liked his books, but he looked, and he looked some more. And then, after he looked for a very long time, after he met a lot of people and talked long into the night with them, after he traveled and spoke with people who lived in those places, why then when he went back to his books he was really smart. If anyone can help us, it's Goldberg."

"When can we see him, grandpa?"

My grandfather shrugged. "He's there, I guess. It's almost on the way home. We'll go knock and see if we're lucky."

"I'm always lucky with you, grandpa."

"You always know what to say, Lily."

"Thank you, grandpa."

Then we walked in silence down 80th street and around the corner past the court with my apartment. We walked around the block. We stopped and I looked across the street. There was water. I stared at it while my grandfather knocked.

The door opened.

"Hello, Benjamin." Mr. Goldberg looked at me. "You're not peddling girl scout cookies, are you?"

I shook my head.

"Too bad. I sit there and eat a box of the thin mint cookies in about two minutes. You come back when you have some to sell me. So, then, why are you here?"

My grandfather spoke up. "Goldberg, we need your brain."

"I didn't think you came here to get me to beat someone up. Come inside."

We walked in. There was an uncomfortable smell. We sat on the couch. My grandfather and Mr. Goldberg talked for a while, and then my grandfather turned to me. "Read Mr. Goldberg your riddle, Lily."

I reached into a pocket and pulled out the paper, and then I read him the riddle.

He blinked twice. I saw him look at my grandfather, who gave a small nod. I suddenly got the idea my grandfather knew the answer, but I couldn't figure out if he did why he didn't just tell me.

Mr. Goldberg made a waving movement with his left hand and said, "Why do you bother me with this? How old are you?"

"Twelve," I said.

"You should be able to solve this. It was written for twelve year olds."

"But..."

He waved his hand. "You know the trick of a magician who makes you look at one hand while he uses the other to do his magic?"

"I guess so," I said.

"This is like that. You're looking at the wrong words. They're meant to trick you.

Don't look at the giraffe, for example, look at the head. And don't think what a ballgame is, think of the word 'ballgame.'"

I looked at the word again. "Okay."

"So what precedes part of the word, not the game?"

I was still puzzled.

"Just look at the first letter of the word."

Then I had it. I looked at the other parts of the clue, and I understood.

"The answer is the letter 'a' isn't it?" I asked.

Mr. Goldberg smiled. "You'll be the only one in the class to get it. So explain your reasoning to me."

"Okay. 'Ballgame' begins with a b. The letter b is preceded by the letter a. In the word head, the letter a is three letters away from the beginning. Finally the letter a is the third letter of the word 'start.'"

My grandfather smiled. He looked very happy.

Mr. Goldberg nodded. "Always feel free to come to me with your puzzles, young lady. But, please, a challenging one next time. About the universe, maybe."

"I'll work on it. And I'll try to get you some girl scout cookies."

We said goodbye, and my grandfather and I walked home.

"Grandpa, did you know the answer?"

"Yes, Lily."

"Then why did we go see Mr. Goldberg?"

"I wanted you to meet him. He taught me a lot. You're getting older now. You will have a lot of questions."

"But you always answer my questions."

"Mr. Goldberg has studied much more than I have, Lily. Between us, you'll get a good education. And, more importantly, he has thought a lot more about God and religion than I have. He's the man to go to for those questions."

I thought about that. When we got home, my grandfather got me a glass of milk and some Oreo cookies. I sat at the table, opened the cookies, and licked the frosting from the inside. As I ate, I asked my grandfather to tell me about the ceremony in Israel for the declaration of independence.

My grandfather was drinking coffee. His eyes raised, and he looked happy as he remembered. "It was a very hot day. Ben-Gurion drove up in his black car. I was with the crowds. Everyone was waving flags. Drivers honked their horns. Now remember, Lily, this was supposed to be a secret ceremony. But everyone knew where it was, and the radio told the country they would broadcast the ceremony, so they gave the time. Some secret. They could have dropped a bomb on the place and all the leaders of the country would not have survived.

"There were a lot of reporters there, a lot of people taking pictures. I had arranged with a friend to take some for me. Ben-Gurion stopped for the photos. The man had a sense of history. He was short, with tufts of white hair sticking out. He never wore a tie. But that day he had a black silk tie and he wore a jacket. We went inside, and I took a seat on one of the brown wooden chairs. There were hundreds of people in the room.

"Ben-Gurion was standing there waiting to read the declaration. Nobody knew it, but Ze'ev, the same man who had recruited Otto for those tasks, was supposed to deliver the declaration, but he was running late. He couldn't find a taxi. So Ze'ev went to a policeman and told him the problem. The man stopped the first car he saw, but the driver said he was rushing home to hear the declaration being read. Ze'ev yelled at him that there would be nothing to hear if he didn't get to the ceremony. So instead of going home, the driver ended up driving Ze'ev and the declaration to the Tel Aviv Museum. They arrived at 3:59, one minute before Ben-Gurion was supposed to start.

"Meanwhile inside, I stared at the Herzl portrait and the flags. I was very proud to have helped. Ben-Gurion finally got the declaration. Then he pounded a gavel and read it."

"Was it on the parchment that Otto and you found?"

My grandfather shook his head. "There wasn't time to copy it, and anyway they had argued about the language up until the last minute. So Ben-Gurion read a typed copy, and he signed a blank parchment. Later they put the words of the declaration on the parchment. After he read it, Ben-Gurion stepped down and started to walk out. Hatikvah, the national anthem was played. I was standing next to a British reporter Ben-Gurion knew. Ben-Gurion stopped, looked at the British reporter, and said, 'You see, we did it.' And they sure did. I wrote a lot of stories about that day."

"Last year in school, I studied about the American Declaration of Independence. Was it the same, grandpa?"

"In some ways it was, Lily. In both cases, Britain ruled the country. But in Israel's case, Britain wanted to leave. In America's case, Britain didn't want to leave. Israel was not so much declaring independence from England as independence from two thousand years of being without a home, independence from having to rely on others for protection. In America's case we wanted independence from a country that wanted to rule us. In America's case it was like a birth certificate. In Israel's case it was like a re-birth certificate."

"I'd like to visit Israel one day. Would you take me grandpa?"

"That's a big trip. But you should go, Lily. You'd like it."

I had trouble sleeping that night because I was excited. I had an idea. There was school the next day, so I had to wait until my walk home to stop and buy a new notebook. Then I went home, opened the notebook, and at the top of the first page, I wrote:

MY DECLARATION OF INDEPENDENCE

I began writing. I thought it would be easy. I'd write that from then on I'd do my own thinking. It was a re-birth certificate, just like Israel's. My grandfather had once told me that we get re-born every day.

I was going to be responsible for myself. I was going to take advice, but not feel like I had to listen to anyone else anymore. But as I wrote, I grew more and more discouraged. The idea had been so clear and so true to me that I was surprised. Independence was a bigger riddle than the ones I had on my treasure hunt. Suddenly I wasn't even sure what it meant to be free. What was I supposed to do?

And it was in that minute that I understood why my grandfather had introduced me to Mr. Goldberg. I knew the real treasures were going to come when I could be satisfied that I had solved the bigger riddles of life, all of which were before me. And I realized I couldn't solve them on my own, that independence required just the balance my grandfather talked about between being a free person and being part of a community. Mr. Goldberg would be there when I needed him, just like my grandfather, and parents, and others.

It was maddening that I couldn't ever separate myself from the world. And even more maddening that I didn't yet really understand the riddles much less be able to solve them.

I sighed, knowing the treasure hunt was only beginning.

CHAPTER ELEVEN:
SHOW BUSINESS

"The principal is going to announce this morning who's singing at the assembly, grandpa. I'm so excited."

My grandfather looked up from his book. "I've heard you singing, my little one. No one is better."

"My father says that, too, but there are a lot of good singers at P.S. 2 and only two are going to be picked."

"Do the others sing like the angel other angels come to hear? Do they have the sweetest face in New York?"

I was finishing my breakfast and feeling good. I didn't answer my grandfather's questions but instead walked over to the school. It was a nice walk. I cut between the apartment buildings on the next block and then went across 21st Avenue to the other side, walked up to 75th Street, and went into the playground.

The day was full of events, and I ran home quickly after school to my grandfather's apartment. He was at a typewriter, and I was sorry that I interrupted him, but he didn't seem unhappy. Maybe he saw my face and knew he needed to hide any feelings of annoyance.

"What's the matter, Lily? You look sad. Aren't you one of the two singers?"

"Not exactly, grandpa."

"What is this, not exactly?"

"David Friedman made it. He's got a great voice, but I didn't think he'd be chosen."

"Yes, and the other one?"

"Laurie Grossman and I have to sing for three teachers tomorrow just before school begins. They're going to pick one of us. I guess they wanted one boy and one girl."

"Then why are you so sad, Lily?"

"Do you know Laurie's father, grandpa?"

He thought for a minute and then shook his head.

I sighed. "He's on television. He sings and he acts. He was in a western just last week."

"I still don't understand, Lily."

"He loves his daughter like you love me, grandpa. I thought Laurie and I would be the winners and sing at the assembly for our families."

My grandfather stayed silent, then he gestured for me to sit down. He went to make a cup of tea. When it was ready, he brought it over with some chocolate cupcakes. We each ate one.

"Are you afraid Laurie will be chosen?"

"I'm afraid if she is chosen and if she isn't."

My grandfather took another sip of tea. "Why do you say that?"

"Grandpa, her father believes in her. She's his only child. She tries her best to please him. If she doesn't win she'll think she let him down."

My grandfather nodded. "Will he be angry with her?"

"Oh, no. He's very nice. She told me he just said she should do her best. He said, that's the definition of a winner, someone who discovers what the best is and does it."

"A smart actor."

"He's very nice, grandpa. That's why I'm sad to beat her, but I also want to sing at that assembly so my family will be proud. What should I do, grandpa?"

"You don't have to do anything, Lily. Just go to the school, sing your best, and let the teachers choose."

I nodded, still not satisfied my grandfather had understood the pain I was going through.

"Remember that comedian, grandpa, the one who wanted to marry your sister?"

"Jimmy Stanton."

"Yes. Is he on tv?"

"A lot, but late at night after you go to bed. He belongs in the middle of the night with everyone in bed."

"He must know what actors feel like. Maybe you could ask him."

My grandfather shook his head. "Jimmy is very funny. A big success. People laugh at his jokes. But he's not a wise man. He lost himself."

"What do you mean, grandpa?"

My grandfather took another sip of tea. "Did you ever hear of the Catskills, Lily?"

I thought for a minute. "Isn't that where mommy and daddy went last year?"

"Exactly. It's in the mountains, You've seen your grandma eating borscht. Well, they called the resorts there the Borscht Belt or the Jewish Alps. These were the places where Jews went, more a few years ago, but they still go. They weren't allowed to go to other resorts so they had their own.

"There was lots of food. And the comedians were crazy. They'd do any wild act for a laugh. They'd jump in the pool. They'd sing after dark when the cars pulled in a semi-circle and turned on their headlights. They could make you laugh for hours. Many comedians started there, many musicians.

"You once told me Jimmy Stanton started on radio."

"And so he did. But he got in trouble once on the radio. He said a joke that wasn't nice. And the president of the cereal company that paid for the show, said he was shocked, and they fired Jimmy. He worked in some clubs in Miami for a few years, and he tried to come back by working in the Catskills."

"What was the joke he told, grandpa?"

"It was an insult to a woman on the show. A personal insult. I can't repeat it."

I thought about that.

"Okay, grandpa. Was he funny in the Catskills?"

"Very. Even I laughed at first. He invited me up there. Sometimes I went with grandma and sometimes not. Remember I was doing writing and reporting, so I wrote about the people who went there, and the entertainers, even the people who worked there. "After a while Jimmy was very lucky. He met a sweet young woman, the niece of the owner of the place he played the most. She helped with the business, and soon she and Jimmy were having dinner every night."

"What was her name?"

I thought my grandfather blushed. I wasn't sure since I had never seen him do that before and I never saw it again. "Her name was Doris, like Doris Day."

"Was she nice?"

"She was as beautiful as a summer morning, Lily. And not spoiled by it. Everyone listened to her. Everyone was surprised she went with Jimmy, but she said he made her laugh."

"Did you know her, grandpa?"

"I interviewed her a few times for my writing."

"Was she as pretty as grandma?"

"Now, Lily, who could be that pretty? Anyway, she made a miracle happen. She changed Jimmy. Or she seemed to change him. He calmed down, became less wild. He began thinking of other people besides himself."

"Did they get married?"

My grandfather looked pained.

"I don't want to finish the rest of the story now. I'll tell you the rest tomorrow, Lily. After you sing."

I hadn't ever seen my grandfather stop a story in the middle like that. I asked him to finish, but he said I should do my homework. I didn't understand why he couldn't continue, but I went back to my apartment.

I had trouble sleeping that night. I lay in bed worrying about what to do the next morning. I kept thinking I could be sick, but I knew that would only delay dealing with the problem. I finally decided to follow my grandfather's advice, do my best, and let happen whatever happened.

I got up the next morning, ate breakfast with my mother, and went outside the apartment to walk to school.

My grandfather was standing on the sidewalk, waiting for me.

"I thought I'd walk to school with you, Lily. Is that all right?"

"Of course, grandpa."

We began. He could still walk quickly, so I didn't have to slow down. After we crossed the street, he said to me, "What are you going to do?"

"Sing my best, grandpa. Just like you said."

He nodded. "You know, you're growing up now, Lily. It's good to listen to other people." He paused and said, "And I don't care what your grandmother says. It's good even sometimes to listen to your grandpa. But, Lily, part of growing up is listening to advice and then deciding on your own what to do."

"What if what you decide is wrong or turns out wrong?"

He shrugged. "You want it easy, don't get born."

We walked in silence until the school. "Good luck, Lily. With your choice."

I hugged my grandfather. I don't cry very much, but I started to sob a bit. I waited outside until I stopped and then went into the school. I walked over to the auditorium. Laurie was already there. The three teachers were talking. I walked up to Laurie.

"Hi," she said. She smiled at me.

"This is terrible," I said. "We're the best two singers. We both deserve to be in the show."

"My father told me show business is never fair."

"I guess not."

The teachers called us. Laurie began. When she finished, I sang the same song.

When we finished, the teachers talked for a few minutes and told us their choice.

Laurie and I nodded, and we walked off to class together.

I half expected to see my grandfather when I left school, but he wasn't there. I stopped off at the candy store, bought twice what I usually got, and then went home. My grandfather wasn't there either.

I had a glass of milk and Oreo cookies. I tried to do my homework, but I couldn't concentrate. Then I went over to his apartment.

He opened the door, and he smiled at me. We didn't speak but walked directly into the living room and sat on the sofa underneath the picture I liked.

"Do you want to talk about it?" he asked.

"I don't know if what I did was right, grandpa."

"Maybe if you say it aloud you'll hear it yourself and decide. I can't decide for you Lily. I can't tell you."

"I know."

"What did you do?"

"I lost, grandpa. They told me I sang the song a little off-key." I wanted to add some words, but held myself back.

"You mean you sang the way your grandpa sings."

I grinned. "Sorry, grandpa. Yes. And mommy."

"At least you come by it honestly."

"No, grandpa. Not so honestly. I sang a little off-key on purpose."

"Oh."

"I don't know who would have won. But I made sure Laurie would."

"Aren't you curious if you would have been chosen?"

I nodded. "Very."

"Then why didn't you try?" My grandfather didn't ask the question in an accusing voice, but in a wise one.

"I thought we both deserved it and I know we both wanted it, but I decided that she needed it more than I did."

"It was a gesture of kindness. That's nice, Lily. But you deserve recognition for your talents."

"I wanted to be nice more than I wanted to be recognized, grandpa."

He nodded. "I'm not sure I would have had the courage to do what you did, Lily."

"Do you think what I did was wrong, grandpa?"

I thought he'd quickly say that he was proud of me, that I wasn't wrong. But he thought for a long time. "Remember, I told you, Lily. You're the one who has to decide that. But since you asked me, in this case, I think what you did was very right."

"Then why did you think about it for so long?"

"Because sacrificing yourself for others isn't always right. Sometimes you have to compete even when you like the person you're competing against. That's what produces the best, when we try our hardest. As long as the competition is fair, you should usually try your best. But here I understand."

"Can I stay for dinner, grandpa? We're having lamb chops and I don't like them. And I want to hear what happened to Jimmy Stanton in the Catskills."

"Do you want to go to that bakery by the library and get some of that new food?"

"Pizza? Sure grandpa, I love it."

"I love it, too, Lily. Come let's go before your grandmother tells me I'm too old for this pizza."

We climbed in his car, and he drove over. We stood in a long line at the window outside the bakery, and ordered our slices. Then we sat in the car and ate them. We had some orange drink in a can that we shared. There was silence and there was chewing, and I don't remember a happier moment in my life.

After the pizza, my grandfather took me to get an ice cream cone.

When we got back, my mother was upset because we had forgotten to tell her we were going, although she figured when she learned my grandfather was gone that we went somewhere together. My mother thought I spent too much time with her father. She thought he was a bad influence. I once heard her call him and say that he told me more than I should know at my age.

My grandfather apologized to her, made some tea, and sat down at the table with me.

"Now I can tell you about Jimmy if you want to hear it."

"Sure grandpa."

"Okay. So the beautiful Doris who had changed Jimmy worked in the business office. She kept the books. She signed the checks, that kind of stuff.

"Jimmy liked to live well. He always would buy people drinks and seem like the big spender. But he hadn't saved much. And for a few months, as I told you, another Jimmy appeared. He was gentler, didn't try to show off, didn't always smoke big cigars, didn't play poker or practical jokes, didn't always brag about how much money he used to make or the famous people he had known. I liked the new Jimmy much better. And he was very nice to Doris.

"They spent a lot of time together. They danced. Jimmy performed and always he would stop and if Doris was in the audience he would walk over to her and tell people she was the woman he loved. Doris had never gotten any public attention before. At first she was shy, and then she liked it, and then she looked forward to it, and then she needed it. So each night, Jimmy would come up with more nice words to say about her. Everyone there thought she was a queen.

"And then I noticed that Jimmy changed back."

He paused. I thought he was trying to decide whether or not to tell me what he was thinking about. Finally, he spoke. "There were a lot of couples in the Catskills, Lily, but there were also a lot of single people looking for a husband or wife or maybe just a friend."

I looked at my grandfather. "Like on tv when they kiss?"

"Yes, just like that."

"We play spin the bottle and kiss at parties sometimes, grandpa."

"Well at the Catskills they really kissed."

"Oh."

"Sometimes there were single women up there and Jimmy kissed them without telling Doris."

"That wasn't very nice."

"No it wasn't. He...."

"He what grandpa?"

My grandfather thought for a second. "He kissed a few married women, too."

"He was bad, grandpa."

"Yes in those ways he was very bad. But he was even worse in another way."

"What's that?"

"He needed money, and he knew that Doris had control over the money, so he told her they needed twenty thousand dollars to start a new life. And she took it."

"She stole the money from her own uncle?"

"Yes she did, Lily. You see, we thought she had changed him, and she seemed to for a while, but at the end he wasn't changed. and he changed her. She stole some money, but he stole what was much more important--her sense of honor, of being good, her own sense of who she was. She abandoned her conscience. Do you understand that?"

"Yes, grandpa."

"And that's why I'm proud of you for what you did today, Lily. You didn't abandon your conscience. Jimmy Stanton was in show business, but the real show business is to show what kind of person you are."

"What happened to Jimmy and Doris?"

"Jimmy was very clever. He had never directly asked Doris to steal. He just kept saying they needed money. When the police came, he told them he meant he'd have to find a high-paying place like on tv. Even Doris, who was furious with him, admitted she had been tricked, that he had been careful.

"So they arrested Doris and let Jimmy go. There was a lot of publicity, and from that Jimmy got a chance on a show. The audience loved him, and he was back on top."

"That's not fair," I said.

"No, it's not. Isn't that what your friend Laurie's dad told her?"

"Yes. It just didn't sound so bad when it was words. It's very bad when it's real. What happened to Doris?"

"I'd rather not say, Lily."

"Grandpa, maybe I'm not grown up yet. But you told me I was old enough to make my own decisions. Don't you think I'm old enough to hear?"

"I don't doubt you, Lily. I doubt my ability to tell it in the right way."

I waited. I think that was the moment I learned about the eloquence of silence.

"She was arrested," he finally said. "Her parents and her aunt tried to convince her uncle not to press charges, but he said she had made a free choice and that she had to pay for it. Anyway, her parents paid her bail.

"The trial was set to begin in September. By a horrible coincidence, it was to start just a day after the first show of a new television series in which Jimmy Stanton had a supporting role. I don't know whether she watched the show that night, but I do know she left her parents' home, drove into New York, went to a large hotel, registered, and went to her room.

"She had a dinner of steak and potatoes and coffee and apple pie."

"How do you know, grandpa?"

"It was in the papers."

"Oh."

"After dinner, she wrote a long note to her parents. She left it on her desk. And then she walked out of the window of the hotel. She was on the nineteenth floor.

According to the paper, she screamed on the way down. She screamed for people to get out of the way. People below looked up."

"Did she die, grandpa?"

"Yes she did, Lily."

"What did she say in the note to her parents?"

"She said she was sorry, that she couldn't stand the thought of going to jail or the pain of how much she had hurt her parents, her aunt, and her uncle. She wrote that she didn't blame her uncle for her death."

"That's all horrible, grandpa."

"Yes it is."

"Did you ever see Jimmy again?"

"Yes. At first I just ignored him, but I kept being bothered. So one night, after he invited me to the show he was in, I went there."

"What did you do, grandpa?"

"I yelled at him, Lily. In front of everybody. I called him a thief and a killer."

"I never heard you yell grandpa. I heard mommy yell, but not you."

"I lost control, Lily. I was Doris' voice for those few minutes and I told him what I thought she would say."

"What did he do?"

"He yelled back at me. But I could see those around knew I was telling the truth. And when I was done, I turned my back on him and walked away. We haven't spoken to each other since then.

"But Jimmy Stanton became famous. He got money and fame but lost his soul. Doris lost her soul but before she died she got her soul back."

"I don't ever want to lose my soul, grandpa."

"I'm glad to hear that, and judging by what you did today, I don't think you will."

I asked my grandfather to walk me back to my apartment and to read a book to me, just like he had done before I could read myself. I fell asleep to the sound of his voice dramatically narrating a story. I don't remember the story, but I can still hear his voice.

I went to the assembly later that week. I enjoyed hearing Laurie Grossman sing. I looked over and saw her father in the audience. His face glowed like it had its own sun inside him.

Almost thirty years later, Laurie called me in the middle of a quiet Sunday afternoon. My family was gathered around the television watching a football game. I was reading.

Laurie and I talked over old times. She told me her father had died the month before. I told her I was sorry. Laurie said she was a writer, married, and happy.

And then she thanked me.

"What for?" I asked.

"I know what you did, Lily," she said. "You let me win. I never told anyone. I should have thanked you then. I should have apologized all those years, but then I would have had to tell my father the truth, and I couldn't face that. I'm not proud of it, but that's the reason I didn't contact you. I'm sorry. But I'm glad I have a chance to thank you now. And I wanted to tell you how much what you did meant to me."

I was silent, waiting for her to continue. Her voice broke a bit as she said, "You taught me that people could be unselfish. I don't think my father would have thought less of me or loved me any less if I had lost, but I know he was very, very proud that day. I heard him on the phone the night of the assembly calling people to tell them how wonderfully his daughter sang. You gave me those calls."

We talked for another two hours about our families and our friends from back then.

That evening, my children asked me why I was singing as I prepared supper.

CHAPTER TWELVE:
THE LIE

It was after the third fight I'd had with my mother in three days that I decided to run away from home. I'd seen young people do that on television, and the idea of breaking away, of living out my declaration of independence, was appealing. I didn't do much preparation. I had some money and put a few clothes in my backpack. I told my mother that after school I'd be going to Nancy Doyle's apartment to work on a science report and so wouldn't be home directly from school. I'd always avoided lying, even to my mother, and so I was surprised at the pleasure I got from telling her a falsehood. I felt a surge of power, as though suddenly my mother didn't have control over me any longer, as though we finally had an equality to our relationship. I assumed I'd feel guilty, or perhaps not even be able to tell her, or lie to her so awkwardly that my mother would detect that I was misleading her and start another fight. None of that happened. My voice was cheerful as I lied to her. And hers was blank as she acknowledged my plans.

I was excited all day, coming to the edge of telling my friends what I was going to do and then pulling back because one of them would have told the teacher or the principal or my mother. During recess, I thought about my grandfather and felt sorry that I hadn't told him, but I knew he would have to tell my mother. It was better this way, I told myself. I'd write when I was somewhere else, tell him I was okay, but never talk to my mother again.

I lingered in the schoolyard at the end of the day. I liked school. I liked the other students, especially. Most of the teachers were all right, except Miss Parsons who had the stiffest back and sternest look that a human being could acquire. Everyone was scared of her. I had her in fourth grade and still shuddered when I walked past her room in the school. But most of the others were kind and tried their best to teach us. I sighed, thinking I'd miss the school.

Instead of walking down 21st Avenue back toward my apartment, I turned right on 75th Street and began to stroll toward Ditmars Boulevard. There was a lot of traffic, much more than on 21st Avenue, and I stopped and just stood there. If this had been one of those television shows I watched, it probably would have begun to rain then, maybe with some thunder and lightning. But there in Jackson Heights it was a bright, sunny day. There were no winds, and the slight breeze was pleasant. There was to be no drama from the sky.

I didn't know where I was going but I kept walking. I stopped at 71st Street. I knew I couldn't walk too much further south or I'd come to the Grand Central Parkway. Going back east meant heading toward home. I wished at that moment that I had planned better. And I was used to getting a snack when I got home. I was hungry. I had assumed I'd buy dinner with some money. I felt as though I had gone over the wall of an escape-proof prison on an island, only now I was at the water's edge after having gotten out, and I didn't know what to do next.

I decided to sit down under a tree to think about it. I realized I should have brought both food and a book to read. I watched the cars go by. I saw a mother walking and holding hands with her two young sons. Sitting there, I felt my anger and its energy gush out of me. Then I thought my confusion came from unfamiliar surroundings. I thought if I walked back, not to my home, but to a spot I knew, I'd be able to think more clearly, to plan where to go. And so I retraced my steps, going back up to 21st Avenue and over to 79th Street. Once I saw the luncheonette, I was hooked. I knew I needed some food, so I went inside.

Mr. Belzer was at the counter and smiled at me. I ordered a grilled cheese sandwich and a chocolate ice cream soda.

"You're all alone today, huh?" Mr. Belzer's face was a sad shade of gray.

"Yes," I said.

"Your grandfather is usually with you. He's my best customer for ice cream sodas."

"He's not here today," I said. Running away had not made me clever with words.

I ate slowly, very slowly. I knew I was supposed to be thinking of a plan, but my mind kept drifting. I was thinking about the science project, about what was on television that night. I could almost hear my mother yelling at me, my father quiet as always, remaining passive. And then I could almost hear my grandfather, not yelling, sitting next to me asking me what was wrong. I pushed my mind back. What was I supposed to do next?

I looked at the clock on the wall. It was almost five. I could still go home, say I'd finished working at Nancy's house. And then I had a bad moment, a horrid moment. What if my mother checked with Nancy's mother? What if Nancy had to go to the dentist that afternoon? I moaned without even realizing it.

Mr. Belzer stopped in front of me. "You don't look so good."

I stared at him and just nodded.

"You want I should call your parents to get you?"

I shook my head. "No thank you, Mr. Belzer."

He shrugged, the most forlorn shrug a human could make.

It was still light outside, but it was starting to get dark. I didn't very much like the dark. Why hadn't I thought of that earlier? Why didn't I find someplace to go before it got dark? Maybe stay with a friend. No, her mother would have called mine if I was going to stay over.

I could hide in one of the cellars behind the apartment building across the street from mine. It faced a field the boys used for baseball. But it was dirty and scary. And darker than the night. And darker than my anger.

I felt paralyzed. The more I sat, the harder it was to get up, or even move. Mr. Belzer had taken away my plate and ice cream soda glass. He was nice, though. He didn't bother me, tell me to move along. The neighborhood was like an extended family, and he was watching out for one of his own.

One lie. It had taken one lie to get me into this.

Mr. Belzer wandered back. "You want my opinion?"

I nodded.

"Call your grandfather. I always ask him what to do and when I do it life turns out okay."

It was a good idea. But I was ashamed. I looked outside and was shocked at how dark it had gotten so quickly.

Mr. Belzer came back with a dime. "The call's on me," he said.

I wanted to tell him that I had money, but the dime was not just a dime, it was him being kind. I accepted the gift, walked to the back of the store, and called my grandfather. I called, hoping my grandmother wouldn't answer, but it was grandfather on the line.

"Hello, grandpa."

"Lily! Where are you? Everyone's looking for you."

I started to repeat the lie and stopped. Then my reflexes took over.

"Why are they looking for me, grandpa?"

"You told your mother you were staying with a friend. That very friend called your home this afternoon and asked to play with you. You lied to your own mother, Lily. Your mother started calling around. She called the school. No one knew where you were. Everyone was in a panic. What have you done, Lily?"

"I've only been gone for three hours, grandpa."

"Lily, you're a young girl from a Jewish family in a tough city. If you're missing for three minutes that is enough time to worry. What happened?"

I struggled to get strength in my voice. "I ran away from home, grandpa."

His voice was calm. "That wasn't such a good idea."

"I'm beginning to think it wasn't, grandpa. Only I don't want to go home and tell mama the truth. She'll yell at me about running away. She'll yell at me about lying. She'll yell at me about being embarrassed at having to call everyone."

"You know your mama, I'm afraid. But you should never lie to her. Lying...." My grandfather stopped talking and remained silent for a long while.

"Grandpa?"

"I'm still here. Listen, Lily, where are you?"

"At the luncheonette we go to."

"Okay. You walk down 79th Street toward Ditmars, turn left, and go one block. There's some street in between. I can't remember the name, but you walk on Ditmars until you get to 80th street. Have you got a pen and paper?"

I took a pen and notebook from my backpack. My grandfather gave me an address.

"You'll see your doctor's office with the sign. The apartment you're looking for is on the same side of the street a few doors down. When you get there, you knock. Mr. Pearlman will answer. Don't be scared of him. I'm going to call him now and tell him you're coming. I'll tell your mama where you are and that I will get you. "

"Who is he, grandpa?"

"He's an acquaintance of mine. Not exactly a friend. But maybe he can help you."

"That would be great, grandpa."

I smiled.

Mr. Belzer looked at me. "See, one talk with your grandfather and you look alive again."

"Thanks for the dime."

"I wish I had a child," he said. It was as though the sadness had left my mind and entered his.

I waved good-bye to Mr. Belzer and began walking again. My legs were more tired than I realized. I heard a dog barking. I was afraid it would attack me. The bark sounded loud and close. I heard it again.

It was very dark, and I was scared. I didn't have far to go, but I usually went with my mother when we came to this part of the neighborhood. The sky looked frightening.

I began to shake a little. Finally, I found the right address and knocked at the door.

The man who opened the door had patchy, red skin. His eyes were sunken, as though they were hiding from the world. He was tall and very thin.

"Mr. Pearlman?"

He nodded. "You must be Lily. Come inside."

I went in, and he led me to the kitchen table. There was a mug of hot chocolate and some graham crackers waiting.

"The writer Hawthorne used to crumble up graham crackers in his chocolate."

I looked up at him. "I didn't know that. I don't even know Hawthorne."

"Ah, he's a writer to read when you get older. If studying him in school doesn't spoil the experience." He paused. "I read a lot," he said, as though that would be enough of an explanation.

We sat mostly in silence. He didn't ask why I was there or about my running away.

My grandfather arrived a few minutes later. He gave me a look, a mixture of relief, bewilderment, anger, and love.

He sat down, exchanged some hellos with Mr. Pearlman, and said, "Davey, I need you to call Lily's mother, and lie to her. Explain that you saw Lily when she was coming home, and she asked you about your story because I had mentioned it. Then apologize. Say she was always safe and because you don't have children you didn't even think that she should call home. You're very sorry. Say I'm here and the three of us are going to eat and then I'm going to walk Lily home."

I looked at my grandfather. "I thought you were angry with me lying, grandpa. I thought you were going to make me tell mama the truth."

My grandfather spoke with me, but his eyes were on Mr. Pearlman.

"I am upset with you, Lily. For many reasons. But for now, let's deal with the moment."

"This will help her?" Mr. Pearlman asked. "This lie?"

"This will save her. You're rescuing her with the lie. She doesn't need to go through this."

The two looked hard at each other.

"You're a philosopher, Benjamin."

"There's no need for name-calling."

Mr. Pearlman laughed. "This was an accident?"

"I didn't set it up. Ask the God you don't believe in if it was an accident."

Mr. Pearlman nodded. I was completely confused. They seemed to be talking in another language, and it wasn't just grown-up.

"This will help me, you think?" Mr. Pearlman looked serious.

"I don't know," my grandfather answered. "I know it will help her."

"That is enough. I'll go call and tell this lie."

Mr. Pearlman got up and went into another room.

"What you did was dangerous, Lily. You could have gotten lost or hurt or worse."

"I was angry at mama."

"Fine, but you have to work out another way to show your anger."

"Like what, grandpa?"

"Like running, or playing basketball, or writing."

"Writing will help if I'm angry?"

"Writing isn't therapy, but it can be therapeutic."

"I don't understand, grandpa."

"Next time you're angry try writing in a journal. In twenty years, you'll thank me because you'll have a record. If you like that you can write more."

"Can I write like you wrote all those articles, grandpa?"

"You'll write better than your grandpa." His voice wasn't sad or filled with the required love a grandfather had. It was serious, as though he meant it.

"You were angry with me about lying, grandpa, but you told Mr. Pearlman to lie."

"Remember I once told you that sometimes there is a higher truth than the literal facts?"

"Yes, grandpa."

"Mr. Pearlman is telling a higher truth. You just told a lie."

"I don't understand why his lie is a higher truth and mine is no good."

"When you understand that you'll understand life."

I thought maybe my brain was going but I didn't understand that either.

Mr. Pearlman returned. "Your daughter is really angry at me, Benjamin. She called me names."

"Stop grinning."

"I liked it."

"You need to tell Lily your story. Otherwise when her mother asks she won't know what to say you talked about."

Mr. Pearlman took a deep breath that came out as a sigh.

"Did you study the communists in school, Lily?"

"Yes."

"I was a communist."

I didn't really understand. To me, this was like saying he was a Martian.

"Way before you were born a lot of people lost their jobs. I went around the country on trains and saw people living under bridges. I heard babies crying in the night for food...."

"It's not a rally, Pearlman."

"Okay, okay. But she should understand."

My grandfather was silent.

"I thought the communists could solve the problems. Treat all the workers fairly. Feed everyone. And so I joined up. Later I became a teacher. Joined Local 5 of the Teachers' Union in New York. I'd write for the communist newspaper, the *Daily Worker*. I'd sign petitions. I thought the Soviet Union was paradise and history would prove I was right."

He paused. "Your grandfather and I were enemies. He opposed the communists and wrote that they were a danger. He wrote about Stalin, the leader of the Soviet Union. We yelled at each other.

"One day, in August, just three years ago..."

"1955," I said.

"Yes, August 16, 1955. A congressional committee investigating the communists called me to testify. I was scared. I liked my job. I was afraid I wouldn't have any money.

"It was terrible. I was under oath. I could have taken the Fifth Amendment, but by then I didn't like the communists so much. I thought I had to tell the truth, or at least part of it. I told them I had joined the Party, but that I had made a mistake, that I didn't understand how bad the communists were, that the Soviets were on our side in World War II. I told them I was very sorry, and it didn't enter my work. I never discussed politics in the classroom. They were happy with that, with my confession, and my saying I was wrong. A lawyer told me to say all that. He told me exactly what to say so that I wouldn't get fired. But then I ran into trouble. The committee particularly wanted me to tell them if any of my friends had been communists. The lawyer said I should name at least one person. But if I did, I was betraying my friends. If I didn't I could go to jail even, and I'd lose my job, or I thought I would.

"What did you do, Mr. Pearlman?"

He looked down.

"Tell her," my grandfather said gently.

Another sigh. "There was a friend in school. Yitz Feld. He had died the previous year. Heart problems. The sweetest man I knew. Very quiet. Very dedicated to his students. He taught them English, specialized in the 17th century. The man knew all there was to know about Milton. Anyway, he didn't have a family, he couldn't suffer. So, I told them he was a party member."

"But he wasn't?" I asked.

Mr. Pearlman shook his head. "He wouldn't know Karl Marx from a grasshopper."

"Why did you lie?"

"I...I wanted to save myself."

"That wasn't nice to do."

"No, Lily, it wasn't. He wasn't around to defend himself. And his students heard. The other teachers. What I did was terrible. I saved my other friends who were members. And I saved myself. The man had died, and I killed his good name that had lived on."

I was still confused. "But why did you want to lie for me?"

"It was your grandfather's idea." He turned around to face my grandfather.

My grandfather said, "I wasn't sure if I was right, Lily, but I knew Mr. Pearlman feels very guilty about what he did. As he should. I wanted to show him that he could use the same weapon he used to do bad and do some good this time. I thought it would help you, and at the same time it might even help him. He might make up a little for doing wrong and see a lie can do some good."

I still didn't understand, but I was glad Mr. Pearlman felt better and that he helped me.

"Thank you, Benjamin. Considering the past, you were very kind to let me do this."

My grandfather nodded. "I hope it helps, Davey."

We walked home. The dark didn't seem so bad at all with my grandfather beside me.

"I hope you understand, Lily. I won't save you from another lie."

"Why did you save me, grandpa?"

He thought for a minute. "I thought you could learn from this, just as Mr. Pearlman did. I thought you could change, and that your mama would perhaps not understand and make the situation even worse." I was surprised by what my grandfather said.

"Will Mr. Pearlman be all right, grandpa?"

"I don't know, Lily. The world is changing. People aren't so scared anymore. Still, Mr. Pearlman needs to do a lot of deeds to make up for what he did. This was one of them."

"I made a bad decision, didn't I, grandpa?"

"Almost. You got to the edge of a bad decision, Lily. But you called me." He hesitated.

"What's the matter, grandpa?"

"Some people, before they make a bad decision, they rehearse it. I'm worried that you didn't run away this time, but that this was a rehearsal for a time when you will run away, when you will make a really bad decision and get into a lot of trouble. I bet Mr. Pearlman didn't become a communist the first time he heard their ideas. But he kept coming back. That first meeting was his rehearsal."

I thought about what my grandfather was saying. "I don't know if I'm rehearsing, grandpa."

"I hope you're not."

When we got home, my mother yelled at me and cried. She said even if Mr. Pearlman didn't know enough to have me call home, I should have known. I didn't yell back. I just listened.

That night instead of watching television, I read a book and then took out some paper and began writing. The words tumbled out of me, more words than I knew were in there.

I didn't know it that night. I had rehearsed, but the rehearsal had not been to run away into the outer world but into the world of language, into books, and literature, and writing. I wrote with a fury.

I saw Mr. Pearlman from time to time in the neighborhood after that, and he always stopped to chat and ask me how I was doing. He told me I had a smart grandfather. He told me that he had learned to help people, and that helped him.

I told him, in simpler words I no longer remember, that I learned that every lie contains its own world, sometimes dangerous, sometimes cruel, sometimes even moral.

And I kept rehearsing, not to lie again, not to run away again, but to learn how to explore all the complex worlds bundled up inside me and inside others.

My grandfather told me that by choosing to explore instead of lying or reacting in anger I had declared my independence from human weakness.

I kept writing.

Mostly I wrote my thoughts in a journal. Or a wrote reports for school

And then I began to write fiction.

When I did, I struggled mightily to write lies that told a deeper truth than facts.

CHAPTER THIRTEEN:
HERITAGE

My father got attacked and robbed three months before my Bat Mitzvah. He was hurt badly enough to have to go to the hospital. My mother wouldn't let me visit him there, but when he came home his head was bandaged. I could see the damage was more than physical. He didn't look at me when he spoke. His eyes were far away.

Friends and family came to visit and console him. The two men who attacked him were not caught, and at night I heard my father tell my mother he feared they would attack him again knowing he carried money. I wanted to ask him to describe the robbery, but I decided not to do so because that would upset him.

For the next few weeks I went to school. It was a few months after I had begun my sentence at Junior High School 141 doing the seventh and eighth grade in one year because I had gotten some score on some test and was in a Special Progress class. The teachers told us not to tell any of the other students that we were in SP classes. A student had been knifed in the school yard during the summer before I arrived. No one ever bothered me, but I didn't like the classes too much.

I got in trouble in an odd way. They gave us achievement tests during the year, and I thought it would be interesting to see if I could answer the reading comprehension questions without reading the passages on which the questions were based. The teacher called my parents because, while I had done very well on the math portion, my reading abilities were measured as only being on a seventh grade level, and I was supposed to be an SP student. My mother asked my grandfather to speak to me about this, and I explained my educational experiment. He seemed amused, and the subject disappeared.

I had to get a ride to school each morning. All those trips were filled with a low level of dread as I slowly realized though never quite accepted that the nurturing atmosphere of P.S. 2 was gone forever. I became more and more distracted in school. My mother and I kept fighting.

And I couldn't stand Sunday school or studying for my Bat Mitzvah which was scheduled for the second week of April. It was the beginning of 1959, and I heard a rumble in my soul that a lot of others must have felt. Otherwise there wouldn't have been the 1960s.

I can feel but not remember the moment they wanted me for a family meeting. I'm sure it was a Sunday afternoon. My mother, father, grandmother, and grandfather and assorted other family members were in our living room. No doubt there was a lot of food, but I don't recall any of it.

My memory starts with me sitting on the couch directly underneath my favorite picture on the wall. I can see their faces, as though they were enlarged and separate from the bodies.

"Lily," my father said, evidently chosen to be the one to tell me the news. "You know what happened to me, and how I feel."

I was cautious. There were too many people with too many serious faces. Was my father dying? Were my parents getting a divorce?

"Yes."

He nodded. Everyone nodded.

"Right. Well, your mother and I have talked and talked, and we've reached a decision that we think will be good for the family."

He wasn't dying. Divorce was still out there.

I sat like a Buddha statue, straining to convey wisdom beyond my age and hide the confusion and anxiety circling around my insides.

"We think your school is dangerous. We think where I work is dangerous for me. The neighborhood is still good, but who knows what that will be like in ten years?"

He paused. I like to think of myself as alert and quick, but I didn't see the obvious coming. My mind just blocked it out.

"Lily, we're going to be moving out of Queens."

I heard it but didn't truly hear it.

"Moving?" I asked. "Who's moving?" It wasn't my greatest moment of mental acuity.

"Us. Our family. Not grandpa and grandma. But our family."

My head felt light. The world began to spin.

I couldn't talk.

"We looked at some places. I had to get a job, too, so we couldn't go just anywhere. We wanted to go to Levittown because so many people moved there. But then we looked further out on Long Island. There's a nice town called Huntington, but the job I thought I had fell through, and we think it's too far out on the Island.

"And then, all of a sudden a few days ago, I learned that there was an opening in Nassau County, and that they wanted me. We are going to live in a very nice community called East Meadow."

"I don't want to move." My voice was gentle but firm. "I don't want to leave Grandpa, or this neighborhood. I don't want to leave my friends." The thought of going where nobody knew me was frightening.

"I understand, Lily, and we're not leaving immediately. I'm going to move out there now to start a job and find a house. You and your mom will move out right after your Bat Mitzvah."

"I'm not going."

My grandfather sat down next to me and turned to face me.

"You know the God we struggle with has provided us with a telephone and a train. And we can write every day. You'll get to be a great writer that way. And I'll save all your letters so you'll remember your life."

There were too many people there to have a talk with my grandfather. I just got up and walked to my room. I sat down and made a list of all my friends, all the people I would probably never see again, all the people to whom I had to say good-bye.

My grandfather knocked at the door about a half hour later.

"Lily, can I come inside?"

"Yes. The door isn't locked."

My grandfather's face was sad. He sat down.

"They've made up their minds," he said. "Your papa has agreed to take the job."

I started to cry. My grandfather just let me sob for a minute.

"Many of the Jews are leaving the cities. They're scared. They want houses and yards. It's called suburbia."

My grandfather shook his head. "I don't think it's so good for the Jews. They won't have neighborhoods. They'll have to drive to get anywhere. They'll meet many new people. That's nice in a way. But it also means that some of our young people will want to marry very nice people who aren't Jewish."

"If you think it's not so good, why don't you tell mama and papa, grandpa?"

"I did, Lily. They did not listen to me. They want to get away, and you have no choice but to go with them." I thought there was a catch in his throat.

"What can I do to help you, Lily?"

I looked up at him. "It's like the whole world came apart all of a sudden, grandpa. I loved P.S. 2, and then I had to go to 141 which is strange to me. I don't like it. And now I have to leave the neighborhood I know. And I have to leave you, grandpa. I can't talk to mama and papa like I talk to you. And I have to leave the friends I like." I showed him my list of friends, and he nodded. "I know what happened to papa, and I understand why he wants to leave."

I looked down. "And all of this comes at such a bad time."

"What else is it that's bothering you, Lily?"

"I can't study for my Bat Mitzvah. Everyone told me it's normal to be nervous, only I'm not nervous or scared. I can learn what I need to learn, and I can say what I need to say."

"Then what's the problem?"

"Religion. It doesn't make sense. They teach the rules but not why I should listen to them. All the questions I have we don't study. Like I want to know how studying this will help me with my life. I ask the teachers, and they ignore me. They just want to teach me about holidays, or more Hebrew words."

"They are looking down at the ground and you want to look up at the sky."

I almost smiled. "Yes, grandpa, I suppose I do. Can you help me?"

"I only wish I could, Lily. But I know who can."

"Who's that, grandpa?"

"Mr. Goldberg."

I thought for a minute. "After he helped me with those questions for the treasure hunt, he did say to come back with real puzzles."

"Indeed, he did."

"But how can he help me, grandpa?"

"Mr. Goldberg is really Rabbi Goldberg, or was Rabbi Goldberg."

"He stopped being a rabbi?"

"He stopped calling himself one, and he stopped his job as one."

"Why did he do that, grandpa?"

"Because he struggled with the questions that bother you. But he's had a lifetime of study and years to think about it. I've had a busy life, and I've read a lot, but he studied and thought about these religious big questions.

"Would you like to talk with him about what's bothering you?"

"Did they fire him, grandpa?"

My grandfather paused. "Why don't you let him tell you the story?"

"Will he answer me or treat me like a little girl?"

"He'll be as serious as you are."

"What if he doesn't have the answers?"

"Oh, Lily I'm sure he doesn't."

I looked confused.

"But no one does. I wouldn't send you to him if he claimed to have the answers, do you understand?"

I nodded.

"He knows the questions, and he can help you think about the answers. He can tell you what you should be searching for, not what you should find. And he can help you judge the answers you do find."

I nodded. "Do I have to move, grandpa? Can I stay here with you?"

"Let's do this, Lily. If you want, you can stay here in the summer, though it's very nice out on Long Island, a little further than where you'll live it is true. Grandma and I will probably want to go out and stay there with you, and perhaps all of us can go out to the beach. But if you want you can stay here. You can come for visits. I promise you, I will be out for many weekends. It's not so far. I've driven on the Northern State Parkway before, and I once even went out to Montauk which is much, much further than East Meadow. Really, it's a pretty easy ride for me. And I can even come out on the Long Island Rail Road. So if you call me, I can be there very quickly."

"Thanks, Grandpa." I sat still for a few seconds. "Why is life so complicated?"

"It gets more complicated every year for me. When I was young there was no television, no this, no that. I don't know. Maybe it's a test. Or a game. Or it's complicated so we don't get bored. Or it's complicated because we're just poor humans and we can't understand why it's complicated."

"Can I see Mr. Goldberg tomorrow after school?"

"I'm sure. I'll call him right now. Meanwhile, maybe it would be a good idea if you went back out and told your mama and papa that you understand why they want to move and you'll help them in any way you can."

"It's good to talk with you, grandpa. You wouldn't be such a good yeller like Mr. Levin across the street, but you're good when I have to talk stuff over."

"Sometimes it's good I don't yell like Mr. Levin, and sometimes not. I am the person I am."

I nodded, and got up to face my parents.

The next afternoon I said good-bye to my friends and walked over to Mr. Goldberg's house. My grandfather was already waiting for me there. Mr. Goldberg and some cookies and lemonade. I had some, and then he turned to me.

"So, Lily, your grandfather tells me you are troubled. That is a good sign."

I looked up at him. "I guess I've got some more riddles to figure out. I'm studying in Hebrew school, and I feel like I'm learning, but I don't understand why or even what I'm supposed to learn."

He nodded. "You want final answers. You've come to the wrong place. I don't have answers."

"My grandfather told me that."

"Your grandfather is a wise man."

My grandfather swept his hand in front of him. "I'm barely literate in Judaism, Goldberg, a simple journalist."

"Nine rabbis can't make a minyan. Ten simple journalists can." Mr. Goldberg turned to me. "I can tell you the right searches to make. I can't tell you what you will find."

"What am I supposed to search for?" I asked.

"Ah, I have a student again. So I will tell you, Lily. The first and hardest search is that you have to discover how to be good. All else flows from that. And then you have to figure out a way to receive God, to understand your relationship to God."

"I don't understand that," I said.

"Every beginning is difficult. You will try one day."

"How will I know I understand God?"

He smiled. "Oy, you're smarter than most of the scholars I know. No one knows God, Lily. That's why I said you have to learn to distinguish right from wrong first. Once you can do that, only then do you turn to God. If you think you understand God, but God wants you to do bad, then you know it's not God."

"Will I be able to talk to God?"

Mr. Goldberg looked startled. He turned to my grandfather. "Did you tell her about Kofsky?"

My grandfather shook his head.

Mr. Goldberg turned to me. "This is a sad story. There are some truths you shouldn't say." Again he turned to my grandfather. "I should tell her this?"

My grandfather shrugged. "It's not so nice. But let her hear."

Mr. Goldberg nodded. "This Kofsky was a friend of ours. Some years ago he was driving to his son to college. They got into a fight, and the son killed Kofsky, stabbed him twenty-one times with a big hunting knife. Someone saw the boy dump

Kofsky's body out of the car, and the witness wrote down the license plate number. The police found the car at the College. The boy was having coffee and talking to his girlfriend.

"Anyway, Mrs. Kofsky, a very nice woman I should say, very kind. She didn't want to lose a son and a husband, so she wanted to have the boy plead insanity. Now I talked to the lawyer, and I asked him why the boy did this killing. And, Lily, the lawyer stared at me and said that the boy had heard the voice of God telling him to stab his father. I don't know to this day whether the boy heard it or it was the lawyer inventing a story to make a case for the boy not being stable.

"The judge must have had pity on poor Mrs. Kofsky. So when the boy ended up pleading insanity, the judge agreed, and the young man was sent to a mental hospital."

"Do you know the real reason why the son did it?"

Mr. Goldberg shook his head. "People are lonely until they find themselves. They get angry at themselves, at God."

"What happened to the boy?"

Mr. Goldberg shook his head again, and added a sigh. "He hanged himself a year later. With his shoelaces. I guess out of guilt. So Mrs. Kofsky lost her husband and her son. Luckily she had two daughters. I think it was those daughters who saved her.

"But, you see, Lily, that's why you need to be sure of right and wrong even if you hear the voice of God, as some say they do."

"How should I look for God?"

"You mean after you have learned how to be good?"

"Yes."

"My advice is to wait until then. But God's house has many doors. Maybe your door will be the same as your grandfather's, through writing. Creating with words is a holy act. I learned from your grandfather that the pen is an ambassador for the heart. Maybe if you write you'll understand your relationship to God.

"Maybe it will be through music or thinking. Maybe it will be through the prayers, and holidays, and the commandments, all that you learn in Hebrew school. But one way or another you will learn what your special relationship with God is and how you and God are partners."

"But why do I need this relationship?"

"Because, Lily, when you can see right from wrong and you find God, you have found the secret of life. All else follows from this knowledge and this relationship. Once you have that you begin exploring the next questions of life."

"What are those?"

"First you need to discover the missions God wants you to accomplish. Then you have to study, to acquire the skills and knowledge to perform the missions. Then you perform those missions. Maybe you finish them, maybe you teach others to continue doing what you have learned. When you finish doing the missions God wanted you to do, then you need to discover your personal missions independent of God. So you put God in the background for a while and study for and perform those missions you want to accomplish in life. And, finally, Lily, you have to discover the missions that both God and you want. And you have to do those. All of these searches and missions are difficult. They each have frustrations and false starts. And there are always temptations to take you away from them. They will take you your whole life.

"This is your heritage, Lily, to learn the good, to find this God we humans have, this God who wants us to do good. And then you have to solve all these questions about what you and God are supposed to do on Earth. This is the Jewish story, this search for God and our moral tasks. We're all partners with God, you see."

My head was dizzy. "That sounds like a lot, Mr. Goldberg. How do I begin?"

"There are hints and starts at every age. You start by learning your tradition. That is the reason you study for your Bat Mitzvah. You learn the rituals even if you don't wish to perform them. And there are missions you must do as a Jew. For some these are the commandments. For most of us, they involve supporting Israel and making sure the United States is strong. For this you need to go to Israel, to be involved in government and politics. You need to help Jews in trouble. For you, from what your grandfather tells me, all of your missions will involve writing. But in all your missions you must never confuse activity with achievement."

I didn't understand what Mr. Goldberg was saying, but I tried not to look confused. His words seemed at the edges of my mind, just beyond my comprehension.

He saw I looked confused.

"Your job is to be a learner. You learn from your parents and teachers what's right."

"My grandfather teaches me that."

Mr. Goldberg smiled. "You have the best teacher. You know, Lily, the word 'Israel' which in this case refers to the Jewish people not the country, means someone who wrestles with God, not someone who believes in God. Your job is to wrestle."

I was hoping for simpler answers, but I didn't say so. I thought maybe I was too young to understand, that comprehension awaited some maturity. Mr. Goldberg was sending me on a complicated and very long treasure hunt.

Mr. Goldberg gave me a book called *God in Search of Man* and said I should read it someday. I thanked him.

My grandfather and I started to walk home.

"Does it get easier when you grow up, grandpa?"

"I think so, Lily, because you can make your own choices. You decide what you want to do."

"If I was a grown-up I'd decide I didn't want to move."

"I know."

"Grandpa, why isn't Mr. Goldberg a rabbi any more? I didn't ask, and he didn't tell me."

We walked in silence for almost a minute before my grandfather answered.

"I don't think he'd mind if I say. Mr. Goldberg couldn't perform funerals any more. He was overwhelmed by grief for the human condition. Since he couldn't do his job, he decided to leave. He wanted people to stop calling him a rabbi."

"I'm sorry, grandpa."

"Yes, so am I. Mr. Goldberg is a very wise man. His congregation was sad to lose him, but they needed someone for all the ceremonies. Many people come to him with religious questions. I don't know so much. Sadly, I don't study the Talmud, but people who do come with their questions. They like his guidance. So his mind works, even if his heart is broken."

That night, as I studied for my Bat Mitzvah, I saw what I was looking at in a new way, as though it were a plan for me, and I had to understand it. The more I read, the more I wanted to read.

My Bat Mitzvah went well. Standing up there I heard rhythms of Mr. Goldberg's voice more than those of my teachers. I felt the ceremony was important for me. It marked the beginning of my search as an adult.

I smiled my way through the reception. I felt more hollow after the ceremony than before. I hoped that wasn't what it meant to be an adult.

I read the book Mr. Goldberg gave me slowly, one page each night before I went to sleep. It read like poetry, and I didn't understand it very well. Like Mr. Goldberg himself, the book seemed beyond me, like a beautiful distant shore I wasn't yet able to reach.

And soon after my Bat Mitzvah, a big van rolled onto 80th street, and some men began to pack our furniture. We all had packed boxes.

My friends came over. Some of us cried and hugged.

My father had driven back to take us, and the ride on the Northern State Parkway seemed long to me. My father pointed out a junior high school on the left side of the highway, and said that would be a sign that we weren't far.

East Meadow was a quiet place. We went into our house, and I went upstairs into my new room. I looked out the window and in the distance I could see some nice clouds. As I requested, my father had set up a bookcase for me. I put my books in it, with Mr. Goldberg's book closest to the bed so I could reach it while I lay down.

I went to school the next day. They were trying me out in the eighth grade because of SP. As I approached my home after school, I decided to go for a walk. The streets were unfamiliar, but I knew further down Front Street almost to Hempstead Turnpike I would find the East Meadow Public Library. I saw a small park across my own street, looked and just started walking. I could have just walked on Front Street but I turned and went street to street. It wasn't long before I got lost. I had a brief moment of panic. Every house and car and tree and patch of sky looked the same. There were some kids outside playing, and I thought of asking them but instead just kept walking.

I was searching in my own way, looking without help for what I needed to find. Soon I felt at peace and just guided myself along. Eventually, I saw an Italian restaurant and knew where I was. I returned home.

My mother gave me an afternoon snack and wanted to know why I was late. I said I had needed to go to the library. She didn't feel like arguing with me and so walked away. I sat and did my homework. Then I went upstairs to my room and looked out in the distance to the skyway that led to someplace far away, some land I did not yet know.

And I was scared that while I had only been lost for a short time on that day in my life I would be lost for a long while. I was afraid that the guideposts that led me back home would be lost, and on some future journeys I would walk around in the fog and the mist of my own confusion, unable to find a way back to myself.

It turned out I was correct. An intense few years of confusion would visit me later in life, and I would go wandering, forgetting for a long while that I had abandoned the only compass that worked. I would forget the true north on my moral compass and get really lost.

CHAPTER FOURTEEN:
TEMPTATIONS

The few years I spent in East Meadow exist in a swirling dark cloud of fights with my mother, endless reading, struggles with writing, isolation, making the phone company wealthy with calls to my grandfather, the unbordered boredom of school, some friendships, and a gnawing, angry desire to break out.

I finally arrived at the summer before I was to depart for college. For the whole of the Spring I had been working on a story. It was about a boy who fights with his father and escapes by watching movie after movie. I wrote it and then started all over with a different boy. Then I re-wrote that story. When I was done, I had written eight versions, changing events and characters and endless words. Finally, I was satisfied. I sent the story to my grandfather. He called and praised me and then spent two hours discussing the story, asking why this character did what he did. I didn't realize writing was so difficult. I thought the words were just supposed to come out and be right. When I was done talking with my grandfather, I re-wrote the story, and then re-wrote it again.

It was finished by mid-summer. My grandfather had suggested a magazine where I should send it and told me about including a cover letter and a self-addressed stamped envelope in case they wished to return it. I prepared both, folded the envelope in half, and put them in another envelope.

But I could not seal it. Each night I stared at my story in the envelope vowing I would mail it the next day, and each night I could not bring myself to do it. I told myself all that could happen if that they could reject the story, and that would be fine. I'd send it somewhere else. But what if every somewhere didn't want it? My future was tucked in the envelope, and I was afraid to send that envelope off into the world.

It was about this time that my grandfather called me. He asked first about the story. I considered lying to him, saying I was still working on it, but finally I told him the truth. He was silent and then told me I would make the right decision. A day later he called me back and announced that he and I should meet in New York. We were, he told me, going to attend a lecture at the 92nd Street Y by the famous author Amos Chaperau, a name his father found more suitable than the Shapiro he had been born with. At the time, Chaperau was, after Isaac Bashevis Singer, the most well-known Yiddish-language writer in America. He was much more beloved in the Jewish community than Philip Roth. He wasn't as good as Roth or Saul Bellow or Bernard Malamud, the big names then emerging in Jewish writing. But he had what all the others didn't have, a friendship with my grandfather.

I packed some clothes and my unmailed story and went to New York.

I met my grandfather, and we took a taxi to the Y. We sat in the Kaufmann Concert Hall with what looked like a thousand other people. I had read the translations of Chaperau's work. There were no dybukks or imps like in Singer. He used an American realism to talk about very Jewish subjects.

He started with a reading of a new short story. The audience laughed, and so did I. Even my grandfather laughed. The story of a broken romance was moving.

After the lecture, we waited while Amos Chaperau talked to people. Then he found my grandfather, and the three of us walked outside to have some early dinner. We found a deli where everyone knew Chaperau and so seated us at a mostly private table in the corner of a back room.

Chaperau was overweight with a few strands of stringy hair looking for companions on an otherwise bald head. He sighed a lot.

We ordered the food—or rather Chaperau ordered for all of us—and then he sat back and looked at me.

"You look eleven."

"I've aged well," I said.

He nodded. "I wish I had. Your grandfather tells me that you write stories."

"I write words. I'm not sure they are stories yet."

He laughed loudly. A few distant diners turned to explore the source of the sound.

"Benjamin you didn't tell me you were bringing along a wit."

My grandfather smiled. "She's more than a wit, Amos."

"Yes, I'm sure."

His face grew serious. "Did your grandfather tell you that I once killed a friend of ours?"

I was startled and couldn't respond.

"It was terrible. He didn't fit. He didn't belong."

"What do you mean?" I asked.

"He was a character in one of my stories. But then when I re-read the story I saw that he didn't belong. So I killed him."

"The character?"

"Of course the character. But characters are no less real to me than people. They are more real. I live with them every day. I speak to them. They speak to me. I killed a man as surely as if it were in reality."

"Was your character angry?"

He nodded. "Very. He came into my sleep and interrupted my dreams. First he begged me to put him back in the story. Then he threatened me, saying I would never find a character as good as he was."

"So what did you do?"

"Why, I'm a pushover. I surrendered. I put him into the story, and that was the story that made me famous.

"That's what you need to be a writer, Lily. You need to be haunted by your characters. And I see by the innocence of your face that you lack part of what you need."

"What's that?"

"You need to go out into the world and taste sin."

My grandfather shook his head. "We've had this argument for thirty years, Amos. She needs to go out and see sin, face it, understand it, and resist it. She doesn't need to sin herself. A doctor doesn't need to break a leg to know how to fix it."

Chaperau gave a dismissive wave of the hand. "If she doesn't know sin, then she won't be able to write. She'll be like someone outside a store who sees others eating ice cream. She can only guess what the ice cream tastes like."

Chaperau turned to me. "Do you know why I write in Yiddish?"

I shook my head. "I assume because it was your native language."

"It is true that we spoke only Yiddish in the house until I was five and went to school. And it is true that my father and grandfather wrote in Yiddish. But that is not why. It is because Yiddish has words, shades of meaning in character that are not in English. The translations of my work are not so good. I know because I do some of them, and I'm aware I can't get the nuances, the precisions of emotion that are carried by the Yiddish. This is especially true in stories of temptation."

He paused. "Do you want to hear a story of temptation?"

I was startled. One of the most famous of American Jewish writers was offering to tell me a story, but one I knew that would make my grandfather uncomfortable. I turned to see what he thought.

He stared into my eyes, and I saw a message from him to me: "It's a story. You should hear it. Listen for the literary lesson, not the moral one."

"Okay, Mr. Chaperau, I'd like to hear your story."

"Good. There is hope for you."

He took a few bites of his sandwich.

"When you're famous, women come to you."

"Amos," my grandfather said.

Chaperau held up his hands. "We're in public. I understand."

"Good."

"Some of these women are quite pretty, prettier than you deserve. You dream about them. You think about them while you drink from your bottle of scotch that is beside your typewriter. They dance before your eyes.

"And then one day, one comes along. She has red hair. You never thought you loved red-headed women before you saw her. But you can't take your eyes off her. Only she is different. She doesn't know she's so beautiful. She just wants to meet you. You are glad to do this. You meet in the park regularly. You sit on a bench and you talk. And she's nice. She laughs at your jokes. She doesn't nag like your wife. She doesn't yell at you like your wife.

"So after some weeks, you begin to think, wait a minute. You think you love this woman with the red hair and the blue eyes and the perfect skin who is very gentle, who always wears black leotards, who talks softly and in her quiet manner wants to hear what you say. Who is so broken by life she cannot talk to strangers, who cannot look people in their face when she talks, who does not believe she has earned the right to be alive. You sit with her more and more often. You stare at her as though she contained all of heaven within her. You don't even understand that she directs your heart away from heaven. You burn for her.

"And one day you are alone at your typewriter, the scotch disappearing faster than the words are appearing, and you think maybe you should leave your drab wife for this red-headed mystery. But then you wonder. Would your talent leave with your wife? You question the Almighty's wisdom in creating a commandment against adultery. You think the heart cannot be denied, but you know sometimes the heart can betray you.

"And so you sit on the park bench. She is coming, this red-headed temptress, this angel, this demon. You have to speak with her now. It is the moment of decision. The words are ready to appear."

Chaperau paused, sipping from his cup of tea.

"And so, Lily, the sinless would-be writer, what would you tell this character to do, stay with his loveless marriage or seek love anew? How would you end this story?"

I looked at him. "Is the red-headed woman Jewish?"

He put his head backwards, opened his mouth widely, and roared with laugher. "No, of course not. This is the new America. This is the America when Jews make the best lovers, the best husbands, the best friends, the best of all of it. Before, Jews had a small selection of jobs, of spouses, of lives. Now they can have it all. This is 1963, Lily. Jews are the new Protestants. Why would they still pick from their small selection? No, the red-headed woman is not Jewish."

I wouldn't let go. "But the man in the story is. He was raised that way. For a thousand generations his family has been Jewish. He's going to give it up for red hair?"

Chaperau looked at my grandfather and then turned to me. "So, all right. He feels guilty. He realizes he has a heritage to preserve. The red-headed woman doesn't know a blintz from a broomstick. The prayers are foreign to her. The guilt about his wife and the distance from the new woman make him determined not to leave for this alluring redhead.

"So, Lily, he stays. And is that the end of the story?"

"I guess not if you're asking."

175

"Indeed it is not. Let me tell you what happens next."

Before he began, Chaperau signaled the waiter and ordered more food. Then he began, "So you're back with your wife. She talks and you don't listen. You yell and she cries. It's a marriage. But then a reporter comes to interview you for a story. You arrange to meet at an expensive restaurant for dinner. Her magazine is going to pay. You show up, not dressed properly but puffing with hope and expectation. You are excited by her, by her endless ringlets of black hair, by bright red lipstick. Here you go again. You tell yourself that chaos is the mother of insight, that success is built on catastrophe. You think as you sigh into her eyes that even fools are sometimes right. You tell her stories you never intended to tell, you speak of private dreams. She listens and sitting there around the time of dessert you are certain you love her. You are ready this time. There is no hesitation.

"You call her the next day and say you need to talk with her again. You ask her to meet you in the park. She tells you she is busy, that she is at that very moment writing a story about you. You ask her why she wants the story when she can talk with you directly. She ignores you and hangs up.

"You think about her all through the day. Everyone has her face. You pace at night. First you can't eat, and then you eat all that is in the refrigerator. You send her flowers and candy. You send her imploring letters. You call again and again. You threaten her, saying you will claim you never said those words if she publishes the story and does not see you again. You have forgotten that she asked permission to tape the interview and did so discreetly. You get angry at her. You get angry at yourself. You are in love with the idea of her more than you thought possible.

"She tells you that you don't know her. That she has a boyfriend. You tell her to leave him and marry you. She asks you gently not to contact her anymore. You are heartbroken."

Chaperau stopped and sipped some water. "Tell me, Lily, do you know the story of Dante and Beatrice?"

"No," I said.

"Dante met her when he was nine. His father took the boy to her house for a party. Beatrice was then eight years old. Dante immediately fell in love with her. According to legend, which I admit is open to question, they met only once more nine years later on a street in Florence. Beatrice was walking with two older women. She was dressed in white. She bowed her head and greeted him. Dante was so overtaken he ran home to think about her. Then he dreamed about her. And only then did he write about her."

"Did they get married?"

"Yes, but not to each other. She was murdered at the age of twenty-four. Dante was married, but Beatrice was his inspiration. He wrote about her all the time even though he could never be with his love."

"That's a sad story," I said.

"Unrequited love is filled with pain. So on with our story. You yearn for this curly-headed woman, but she doesn't like you. You're miserable, but you go on with your life. You go through your daily chores, but thoughts of her at always at your side.

"And, so, Lily, is that it? Our hero has lost his love and lives out a miserable existence?"

"That wouldn't be a good ending."

"Perhaps. Maybe it is. But if you don't like it, and therefore we will continue. So you go on, unhappy, dragging yourself through a fog that comes with each day. You try to write and spend your time sighing.

"And then, life decides to charm you again. In the morning you're miserable, and in the afternoon you meet another woman."

"That's a lot of women."

He shrugs. "It's a big city. This woman arranges for you to speak. You like her voice on the telephone, and you agree. You go to speak. Most of the people there are old women who decide their lives are interesting because they've heard you read. Your new book has just been reviewed in the *Times*, and everyone wants to touch you. So this new woman, she doesn't wear bright red lipstick. She's got straight hair. She's tall and thin. You like her serious face. Your curly-headed Beatrice goes out of your head. You have a new toy to play with.

"You call her the next day to thank her, and ask her to go for coffee. She is embarrassed, but she agrees. You meet for coffee, and she is charming, new to the city, from a small town in Pennsylvania. You ask her to read a new story you've written, and she's overwhelmed. You've translated it for her, of course, but she doesn't know that.

"Now she is the one who receives your flowers and candy and calls. She is star-struck. You are again ready to leave your wife."

"If I was the wife I'd already have clobbered the guy with a heavy rolling pin."

Chaperau smiled. "Don't think she doesn't ponder it. But she's too scared to act. Anyway, you are again at a decision point. And, again, Lily, I ask you what happens now in the story?"

"He really leaves."

Chaperau was silent for a moment.

"I'm surprised you say that. But, all right, the end is yours. You leave your miserable wife. You move in to a cramped apartment with your new love. All is good for the first several weeks, and then you realize she is strange. In the story it is not necessary to know how she is strange, but she is very strange. You are scared. You think maybe you made a mistake. But you can't go back. You can't stay. You realize maybe the love you searched for and then got wasn't so good for you. But you are trapped."

"I don't understand the story," Lily said.

"It's about the Jews in America," my grandfather said.

Chaperau threw up his arms. "It's exactly the Jews in America. They keep being charmed by the place. They love this. They love that. They decide to leave their old ways. Sometimes America loves them. Sometimes not. And, now, just when they find the embrace they so longed for, they realize slowly, and some never, that the embrace was not so good.

"They see what they get from America, not what they give up." He sighed. "This is my problem, too. I am blind to what I am giving up, even as I embrace my fame. This story is my warning to you, Lily. You will meet many temptations in this Babylon. Watch me, for I surrendered to them."

We finished in silence, and my grandfather and I went to get a subway back to Queens. I would stay overnight and then go back on the train in the morning.

As the subway cars rumbled along, my grandfather said, "He's quite a man, but underneath he means well."

"I know that, grandpa."

It was after we got off the subway and were walking that I turned and said, "Why did you bring me to meet him, grandpa?"

"You need models to see what you want to be like and what you don't. Right now, you're rehearsing for adulthood."

"You don't want me to be like that, do you?"

My grandfather shrugged. "You're too old to be what I want you to be like. You have to decide. But I will tell you that Amos is right. There are many temptations in life. I don't think Amos has made the right choices all the time, and I think he doesn't think he's always made the right choices.

"But there is a temptation you had that I didn't like, and I wanted you to think about that."

"What is it?"

"It's your story, Lily. You worked very hard on it. You re-wrote it. I'm very proud of you for that. But then you didn't send it. You were tempted to give up on yourself before you even tried. You'll meet many obstacles. There will be many times when you want to give up. That's as big a temptation as the women in Amos' story. Giving up can be as appealing as that red-haired woman.

"But there are miracles in every breath, Lily. Who knows what will happen during your million tomorrows?"

"My father wants me to be an accountant."

"Is that what you want to be?"

"I don't know what I want, grandpa. I know I want to write, but that's not a job except for a few people."

"It's not so easy to take off the harness others put on us."

"I know why I can't send the story, grandpa. I'm scared to fail."

"So am I, Lily. It's part of being human."

"Will you think less of me if I can't sell that story?"

"I'll never think less of you, no matter what you do. The question is whether you will think less of yourself if you don't send it, if you give in to the temptation of not trying because that's easier."

My grandfather made us both cups of hot chocolate that night and we spoke. I told him I was both scared of college and yet desperately wanted to go. All my fears were turned into words that night as I gave voice to them. My grandfather didn't have too much advice. He simply listened.

I couldn't sleep. I kept pacing, thinking of Chaperau, thinking of myself.

I slept fitfully, and woke up about 8:30. My grandfather was already up, reading the paper.

"Will you come for a walk with me, grandpa?"
"Always," he said. "Where are we going?"

"To the post office."

CHAPTER FIFTEEN:
THE WALL

I planned to visit Israel for the first time during the summer after I finished my master's degree. It was 1968 and the year before Israel had gained control over the Western Wall in Jerusalem. I had read about the Wall and wanted to see it for myself, to touch its stones and to put a note in it. My original plan was to go alone, but then an event occurred the April before I planned to go that made me change my mind.

I had seen my grandfather less over the previous two years. I still hadn't sold any of my writing, but I kept getting little notes from editors telling me that they liked what I wrote. Sometimes they asked me to send another story, and many encouraged me to keep writing. I tried, still without success. I was becoming discouraged and decided I would be better off focusing on completing my education and getting a job.

I learned about what happened from my mother. Her voice was calm as she called to tell me that my grandfather had suffered a heart attack. He was going to be fine, she assured me. He was already home and resting after the operation. She had waited until she knew that before she let me know. I was annoyed she hadn't let me know immediately, but this was not the time for another fight.

I went to Queens that afternoon and rushed over to see him. He looked pale, his skin a color I had never seen it. My grandmother and mother kept him supplied with soup and all else he wanted. He had a pile of books and magazines nearby, and a radio.

He saw me enter the room and signaled me to approach. He looked at me, and I knew that he understood what I had not said.

"I'm fine, Lily, so why are you here?"

"Very funny, grandpa. You're lying sick in bed, and you joke with me."

"Ah, you have to laugh at death. For dying, you always have time. Tell me, how is your college?" My grandfather was always sorry that he had not been able to go to college, but he had read more books than any college graduate I knew.

"My college is standing there, doing well." I was getting a degree in sociology, and so far had no idea what I was going to do with it. I kept going to the office that handled interviews for jobs and looking. I kept reading about jobs. I did all I could except find a job. I couldn't even think what I wanted to do. All the sociologists I knew just taught sociology.

"The doctor said he should be as healthy as I am."

I sat down beside my grandfather and took his hand. Suddenly I began crying.

He looked at me and said, "Save this ocean for my funeral, Lily. I tell you I'll be stronger in a week than I was before. They fixed me up. I had a good doctor. Of course some of the others, oy. If they kiss a nurse, she should count her teeth. My good doctor gave me a diet and some exercises. Exercises. Whoever heard of a seventy-eight year old man exercising?"

"But you'll do it, right, grandpa?"

"Yes, yes. I'll walk all over Queens. I'll trot over to La Guardia and welcome the incoming flights. I'll beat the cars as I cross every street."

My grandfather was going to be all right.

He did get strong very fast, and a month later when I visited him again, I was amazed at his robust appearance. He had lost some weight and looked five years younger.

"Ah," he said to me, "Now if only I had some interesting places to walk."

That was the moment it hit me. "Grandpa, I have a strange idea. I'm going to Israel this summer, maybe in late July. Do you want to go with me? There are great places to walk, especially now. We can see all of Jerusalem, and we can go on the Golan Heights."

He perked me. "Another trip to Israel. I have many sights to show you, Lily."

"Good. Let's plan to do it, grandpa."

He got the go-ahead from his doctor who said he thought such a trip would be beneficial. My grandmother was pleased that he was going. I wasn't quite sure why. And so we planned. We looked at the El Al flights. We decided to stay first at the King David Hotel in Jerusalem, and we got a travel agent to book us in various places.

And so it was that in mid-summer I walked into my room at the hotel. My grandfather's room was next door. I wanted to be near him in case he needed me.

For the next week we traveled the country. We spent overnight in Kfar Giladi on a kibbutz. It was right near the border with Syria and Lebanon, and when I saw that the guards looked about eleven I got scared. I was surprised at how good the food tasted. I rode a camel for the first time—and the last. We went to the Golan Heights. Our guide said he had fought right there, and asked if anyone in the group wanted to walk across a minefield to stand in what had been a Syrian bunker. My grandfather and I were the only ones who wanted to do so, but we were careful to walk in the guide's exact footsteps.

The next day my grandfather asked if I wanted to spend a day on an archeological dig, and I agreed. We arrived. After a brief tour, one of the men there asked us if we wanted to explore underground, to crawl through to the area where they found an amazing room. My grandfather stayed above ground, but I decided to go.

I hadn't expected what I found. I got on my belly. There was barely any room on other side and not much above me. A small group of us began to crawl along. I was right behind the leader, and after about ten minutes of crawling through the darkness, an unbearable urge to ask him a question took over my mind.

"What happens," I asked him, "If someone, I don't know, goes crazy down here?" It was very easy for me to imagine that.

"We stop," he said, "and I crawl over people and take the person back while everyone else waits here." I silently prayed that no one would go crazy.

We crawled some more. The leader stopped and pointed to a passage on our left. "Don't anyone go down there. We don't know where it leads."

I shuddered.

We kept going. It was now about a half-hour crawling along. All of a sudden, the space narrowed. I squeezed through.

"What happens," I asked, "If someone gets stuck?"

"It happened yesterday," he said.

"What did you do?"

He shrugged. "Some people pushed, and some people pulled, and the person got loose."

I was not reassured.

After about forty minutes of this, the leader stopped. We couldn't see ahead.

He turned to me. "There's a short drop here. Just jump off."

I peered ahead. There was, as far as I could tell, infinite darkness. "You want me to jump down there?"

"Yes. Don't worry. It's absolutely safe. It's just a short drop."

No one in Israel, so far as I knew, had a motive to do me any harm. So I jumped. And it was just a short distance. Then we crawled some more until we got into a large room filled with many crevices in the rock.

When we got back out, my grandfather asked how I enjoyed it.

"I can't believe people used to live there," I said.

"They needed to escape the heat and the animals," he said.

"I'm glad I'm living now."

I felt like going through the cave had been some kind of test, some passage. I had gone in one way and come out another, only I didn't understand what I was at either the beginning or the end. I just knew I was different.

We went back to Jerusalem. I was now ready to visit the Wall. There was a message waiting for us at the King David.

"Hmm. Lily, you remember my relative, Yaakov?"

"Of course, grandpa." I hadn't seen him since the sixth grade, but I would never forget him and his stories about the Holocaust.

"He's forty-one years old now, and he is in Israel this whole summer. He wrote to me, and your grandmother wrote back to him to say we were here. And he has invited us to lunch tomorrow."

We spent the morning walking through to the Western Wall and shopping in the Arab stalls. My grandfather said the owners would be disappointed if I didn't argue over the prices. I soon learned the rules of the game, and had a lot of fun buying some scarves and also some jewelry. They took American credit cards and were happy to do so.

We got to the Western Wall around ten in the morning. It was beginning to get hot. I put one of the scarves over my head. There was a men's side and a women's side. I went way to the left on my side, and my grandfather way to the right on his, and so we were very close to each other.

I said a prayer and touched the stones. I had never undergone any religious experience at all like the ones I read about. But when I touched the stones at the Wall, I felt what seemed to be almost an electric shock. I put my hands on it again, and they felt attached to the Wall, almost part of it. I felt a charge, as though some kind of message was being sent to me. I didn't understand the message. It wasn't in any language I grasped. I quickly wrote a prayer on a piece of paper and put it into one of the crevices.

I asked my grandfather about my reaction to the Wall on our way to meet Yaakov. He said he hadn't had such a feeling, but that maybe God was reaching out to me. Maybe, he said, like in the book Mr. Goldberg had given me, God was in search of me.

I pondered that while we walked.

I didn't quite recall what Yaakov looked like, but the man we met was smiling, beaming even, completely different from the man I remembered.

He asked about my grandfather's health, about our trip, about my plans for the future. And then he said, "I've got a story to tell both of you."

He paused to take a drink of water and turned to me.

"Lily, it's been a long while since we spoke. Do you remember me telling you about my wife?"

"Yes," I said carefully. I didn't want to mention that she had been a victim of experiments or couldn't have children.

"Good, so you'll understand this story. My wife and I came here a year ago, just after the Israel army had liberated the Wall. It was now finally back in Jewish hands. I was so excited that when we arrived at our hotel on the first night I couldn't sleep. My wife was exhausted, but I had to go myself to the Wall immediately.

"It was dark, colder than I expected. I got there and there was only one young man there, a boy really. I stared at him because he looked just as I had looked before I went into the camp. He had the same gaunt face, the same thin beard, the same dark eyes.

LAWRENCE J. EPSTEIN

"He came up to me. We said hello. We talked a bit, and he said it was a custom to write a prayer to put in the Wall. I explained that I knew that, but I didn't want to pray. I didn't want to explain to him my anger at God about not having a child, about having a wife given a lifelong sentence to be without a child. I didn't want to tell him that I had stopped praying, but that I wanted just to see the Wall because of its history.

"But he wouldn't walk away. I kept refusing and he kept pleading with me to write a message. Maybe if he hadn't looked like me as a teenager I would have left or just ignored him. But I couldn't.

"I took the paper and pencil he gave me. I wrote the prayer 'I want a baby' in Hebrew and folded the message. Then, with tears in my eyes, I put the piece of paper in the Wall and stayed there. With what I had seen in the camp what did I have to say to God? All I would do would yell and scream. If there was a God that is. I didn't know.

"After a few minutes, I turned around, and the young man was gone. I looked all over for him, but he was not to be found.

"And now when I go to the Wall, I look for him, but I never see him. Sometimes I think he was a ghost or that I imagined him. But I still look."

Yaakov stood up. "Come," he said, "My wife yelled at me. She said you are not to leave Israel without seeing her."

We walked to a quiet Jerusalem neighborhood into the small apartment Yaakov and his wife had rented. She was a tiny woman, maybe a year younger than her husband, with the sweetest smile. She hugged me when we were introduced.

Then she brought out some honey cakes and tea. We ate. Yaakov looked at his wife and said to us. "Come to the next room."

We got up. He led us inside. There was a baby sleeping peacefully in a crib.

"It's a girl. She was born ten months after I put that note in the Wall." Then he turned to me. "Tell me, Lily, now what am I supposed to say to God? Am I supposed to yell or say thank you or both? Am I supposed to believe in God or not?"

"I don't know," I said.

"The wisest words possible," he responded. "Who knows? Maybe it's true that God is closest to those with broken hearts."

We stayed and asked about the baby, about their plans. Yaakov said they were going back to New York but would visit Israel often, that his baby was a gift from Israel, from the Wall.

My grandfather and I stayed in Israel for a few more days. I went back to the Wall twice more, but I didn't feel that electric charge again.

It was on our last night in Israel when my grandfather got a call in his room at the hotel. He knocked at my door.

I could see by his face that tragedy had visited somewhere close to him. He walked inside and before sitting down he said. "Your grandmother has died."

I stared at him. "What? I didn't know she was sick, grandpa."

He shook his head. "Neither did I. Neither did she, or she didn't complain about it. Your father and mother are taking care of the arrangements. They know who to call. They'll wait an extra day until we get back and other family members can come to New York."

"I'm so sorry, grandpa."

He looked so alone, so forlorn. I asked him if he had any tasks for me, even minor ones, any shopping I needed to do, for example. He simply shook his head.

"Lily, is it all right if I go back to my room and just lie down? Sometimes sleep is the only available escape."

189

"Of course, grandpa."

I went downstairs in the King David, to the desk on the left to leave my key, and then out the front door. I just started walking. I remembered once a rabbi had told me that the only people who are dead are those who have been forgotten, but the words that sounded so good when he spoke them now struck me as insufficient. A pain ran through me. I knew my life wouldn't be the same again, and, much worse, I knew my grandfather's life wouldn't be the same again.

I remembered the stories he told me and wondered if he'd be there to tell me more, to introduce me to the characters he knew, people who were alive. I thought of the romances I had had myself, and how they always disappointed me because they were so shallow, so empty of any meaning.

I looked up when I almost bumped into a young child. Several boys were around me trying to sell me stuff they promised was genuine. I was in the markets. I headed through them toward the Wall.

It was crowded when I got there, filled with American and European tourists. I waited in the back until the crowds thinned and I could find a spot to touch the stones again. I found myself next to an elderly woman, about the same age as my grandmother. I pondered the mystery of why this woman was alive and my grandmother wasn't. She was dressed like an American and nodded to me as I stood next to her.

"You speak English?" she asked.

"Yes," I said. "I'm from Long Island."

She nodded. "Buffalo. We're practically neighbors."

I smiled.

"My husband died," she said.

"I'm sorry."

She nodded again. "Thank you. He was old. On his deathbed he said to me that it was never too late to lead my life.

Since I was a little girl I dreamed of visiting the Land of Israel. You're lucky to be here when you're so young."

"I am," I said.

"I tell fortunes," she said. "If you give me your hand I'll tell your fortune."

"Go ahead," I said, sticking out my hand, pleased that I could make her feel useful and amused at her efforts to predict my future.

She began pulling her finger over the lines in my hand. "I'm sorry. This one means great sadness. We shall not speak of it, for the other lines are filled with the sparks of life. Oh, you shall live a long while, and have children, may they provide you with great joy. This line says that you are a searcher. Oh, my." She stopped.

"What's the matter?"

"It's not terrible. It just says, never mind what it says. I say to you if you don't love what you do, you have nothing. It may take many years but you must keep searching, and you will find it. Some find it as children, some never. You will find it later, so you must keep searching."

I shook my head. "I don't understand."

"I only read the lines in your hand and speak to you. It is up to you to understand."

"I should keep searching."

"Yes. You will see signs. You will think you are unhappy, but you are really searching."

She let go of my hand.

"You don't believe in this nonsense, do you?" she asked.

"I didn't. But what you said was very interesting."

"It is just a conversation. I just read palms. Many people did it when I was a child. People believed it. They thought an astrologer or a reader of palms or tea leaves could direct their lives. They were lost and scared. But I learned by doing it to understand people. Do you know what I'm saying?"

"Yes."

"Good. Forget the palms. Consider the words."

"Thank you."

She went back to praying.

The next day, my grandfather and I flew back to the United States. We were mostly silent on the trip. I kept playing the sights and sounds of Israel through my imagination.

The funeral was dignified. The rabbi knew my grandmother well and had kind words to say about her. My grandfather was unable to speak, but my father spoke for the family. I felt tears well up within me. I could almost feel their path inside me until they found an escape into the world.

I've learned over the years that I could get used to funerals, to accept them. But sitting there then I could not accept that my grandmother was gone, that my grandfather's life would have an unbearable emptiness.

I thought of Yaakov's new baby. A life begins and a life ends. And in between, if the old woman at the Wall was right, all I could do was search.

And that was that. Suddenly I sat erect. There was some force being roused inside me. I felt a fire in every vein. I determined to charge toward my future. I knew to expect tragedy and pain, and I knew I would find disappointment and would wander down wrong alleys. I feared I would throw rocks and injure other Dennis Bellos in my life.

But, most surprisingly, even shockingly, on this day, I made a vow. I was determined to seize life, to taste it. I was determined to keep searching, to touch mystery with one hand and hard reality with the other. I would be like Israel and never let history defeat me. Whenever I tasted defeat, I would always return to life.

I saw an image that afternoon. I watched it form in my imagination until it filled my mind.

I would walk with the spirit of the Wall inside me.

I stepped outside and took a look around.

CHAPTER SIXTEEN:
FAMILY

My grandfather was never really the same again after his wife died. He told me he was all right during the day, but the nights were long, dark, and painful. I asked him if he considered remarriage to blunt the loneliness, but he just shook his head. I thought that for the only time I'd ever seen, he seemed defeated by life.

I was forging ahead in my own life and, while I felt guilty at ignoring him, I didn't see him much. I called him at least once a week, often more frequently, but the conversations over time became trite, empty of the zest, a shadow of the relationship we always had.

That is, until I needed help with two problems. They came together a couple of years after our trip to Israel and my grandmother's death. I had discovered the truth many students who do well in graduate school discover, that it's a pleasant way of life, that seeking a job and then having a job is a very painful alternative, and that everyone praised me for being a student and doing well at it. I therefore had stayed on to get a Ph.D. in sociology, a field I liked less than I told people because so much of the work we did involved statistics.

To distract myself, I began doing serious genealogy. I sent for passenger records. I looked into the National Archives. I discovered the Mormons were sophisticated genealogists because of their religious teachings and that they had compiled much interesting information. There wasn't much then to read in Jewish genealogy, so I was mostly on my own. I did contact YIVO, where Yiddish records were kept, and similar repositories.

I was stuck on my father's father. I knew his name and that was all. He had died when my father was a child. My father only had a vague memory of the funeral and didn't know where he was buried. I was particularly interested in learning which town in Europe he had come from. I decided to ask my grandfather for help.

It was while I was working on the genealogy that a close friend studying sociology with me became disheartened. She came to me for help. I had been friends with her since we were sophomores and, as friends are, we were intimately familiar with each other's interests, romances, faults, and tastes. It was her romance that was a problem. There emerged a moment when I needed advice.

I took both problems to my grandfather. He had by then left his apartment and was living with my parents in East Meadow. He had not wanted to move in with them, but they built an addition with a separate entrance to give him a private apartment. My mother cooked for him each night, took him on his too frequent visits to one doctor or another, and generally looked after him.

I arrived home late one Friday afternoon. He was sitting in the backyard when I walked outside.

"All of nature is yours now, grandpa."

He looked up. "You and Thoreau can have it. I'll take the crowded city. The sun doesn't need my help to set."

"I guess my plan of building you a pond is out then."

"Build me a library."

"Grandpa, I came for some advice."

I may have deceived myself. Maybe it was the sunlight in my eyes. But at that moment I could have sworn that my grandfather looked better.

"I've read a bit of sociology."

I shook my head. "No, not with school. I need help about searching for my other grandfather, and I need to make a moral decision."

"A moral decision presses on the mind."

"It does on mine. I have a friend at school, grandpa...."

"Wait, is this a real friend or an invented friend so you won't have to tell me what you did because you're ashamed of it?"

I smiled. "This is a very real friend. You know her. It's Annie O'Neill."

"Ah yes, a very wonderful young woman. A very nice smile."

"That's her, grandpa."

"So what has happened to Annie?"

"I don't know if you'll like the story, grandpa."

He made a dismissive shrug. "You're not going to shock me, Lily."

"It's not shocking. Annie just fell in love, that's all. It's who she fell in love with and who loves her that might disturb you."

"Ah, one of our people, yes?"

"You're not kidding. His father is a rabbi."

"So the first problem for Annie is to know whether her young lover is really in love with her or simply in a rebellious stage against his father."

I hadn't thought of that. Isaac was a rebellious kind. I thought about it for a minute.

"I don't know."

"Okay. So tell me the problem."

"It's a long story."

"Do I look like I'm ready to run off?"

"No, you look like you're enjoying nature."

"You used to be such a nice little girl."

"I'm sorry to disappoint you, grandpa."

He waved his hand again. "It's your nature that disappoints me. You, I'd be disappointed if you didn't know how to talk.

Okay, so your lovely Catholic friend is in love with a rabbi's son. Tell me your story."

"Okay, grandpa. So they knew there were problems. They both talked about it. But love doesn't always cooperate. The more they spoke, the more time together they spent, the more they knew they had found their true love. They didn't want to separate.

"So, they agreed to get married. It was only then that they had to tell their parents. Isaac went home for a Shabbos dinner. They ate in peace, and afterwards Isaac sat down with his parents and told them he was in love with a Catholic woman.

"They were horrified, grandpa. His father asked him if he knew such a move would put the rabbi's job in jeopardy. He said no one in the family had ever intermarried, and his own parents, if they were alive, would have dropped dead on the spot. After a half hour of yelling, Isaac's mother had an idea. She offered him $5,000 if he would forget all about Annie and look for a nice Jewish girl to marry.

"He told them that he was offended. That he wasn't for sale and they couldn't put a price on true love.

"Then his father had an idea. He said Isaac should move to Jerusalem for eighteen months. He should study the holy texts at a school there and not be in touch with Annie. If, after that, his father said, Isaac still wished to marry Annie the family would not stand in his way.

"Isaac was torn. He certainly did not want to leave Annie for a year and a half, but in the crazy scheme he saw a solution. They would delay but then have a lifetime of married life with his parents' approval. He pondered all this.

"Meanwhile, Annie had gone to her parents. Her grandmother was there, and she started to scream. She said some terrible words about Jews, grandpa."

"There are many such terrible words."

"And she knew them all. They said they would never talk to Annie again if she married a Jew.

"Why is there so much hate, grandpa?"

He shrugged. "Some of it is hate, yes. But it's a mix. Some of it is confusion. And a sense of being rejected as parents. There are many emotions. And I admit that both sets of parents acted wrong in this case. But they were protecting what they thought important. You have to see that too. A real dilemma is not right versus wrong, Lily, it's right versus right. It's right to be in love, but it's also right to realize you're not just an individual, you're part of a people."

"I suppose. Anyway, they got together to discuss what Isaac's parents had demanded. They both cried, but decided that despite the pain they would both feel, they could write long letters to each other. They could even see a romantic side to that, for they could keep those letters forever, show them to their grandchildren.

"Isaac agreed to his father's condition. A week later Annie drove him to the airport. He flew to Jerusalem and began study in a yeshiva there.

"There's one other person involved in this story, grandpa. Annie has a younger brother named Jimmy. He heard their fight. He'll be important later on in the story."

"I'm not overly senile. I'll remember him."

"Sorry."

"Okay, so Isaac is in Switzerland." He paused. "I'm kidding. It's old people humor."

"It's not funny, grandpa."

"You have to learn to live, I have to learn to die. You're coming of age. I'm coming of old age. It's life. Go on. Isaac's in Jerusalem."

"This is the part of the story I only know from Jimmy. He called me yesterday to tell me. I have to decide what exactly to tell Annie. Or maybe how to tell it."

"Go on."

"This is terrible, grandpa. I'm angry just saying it." I paused.

"Anyway, after Isaac left the two families met. They were united in their desire not to have the marriage go through. They agreed on a plan that was secret. Jimmy wasn't supposed to tell me.

"Their plan was to hide the letters that Isaac and Annie sent to each other. They started like that, and then it got much worse.

"Isaac wrote every day. It was Jimmy's job to intercept the letters and give them to his mother. She destroyed them. She didn't want to take a chance that Annie would find them anywhere. Soon, Annie became disturbed. She kept asking her parents if she had heard from Isaac. They lied to her and told her he had never written a single letter.

"She kept writing to him. But since she didn't have Isaac's address in Jerusalem, she had to deliver them to his parents' house. She left them by the side of the door. You can imagine what they did. Obviously, none of the letters was mailed.

"Then there was a moment of panic. Isaac announced that since he hadn't heard from Annie, he was flying back to the United States. The parents spoke and they came up with a plan. Annie had always wanted to visit Italy because she loved Italian art. Her parents said they would send her there and maybe there would be a letter from Isaac when she got back. They made arrangements for her trip to be just when Isaac would be back in the U.S.

"Poor Isaac. He arrived, went to Annie's house, and was told the truth, that she was traveling overseas. But then they lied and said she had stopped talking about him, that she seemed to be interested in another young man, a good Catholic. They said she must have realized an intermarriage would not work out. Distraught, Isaac left several letters with them. They destroyed the letters as soon as he walked out the door.

"Isaac went back to Jerusalem and Annie returned home."

"These are some parents. They should go to the Parents' Hall of Fame."

"I know, grandpa. They were terrible. Only they got worse."

"Oy. How could they get any worse?"

"Remember, I only know this from Jimmy. He kept track of it all. He even wrote it down in a journal. A few months went by, and then Isaac's parents wrote him a letter. They said Annie had gotten married and that she was expecting a baby. This was, of course, a completely invented lie.

"Isaac was broken-hearted. It is on the basis of evidence in letters he sent to Annie's parents that I can construct what happened next.

"Oh, grandpa, it's terrible. He thought Annie had married. So he really did marry a woman in Israel. He didn't love her. She had a young son. Her first husband had been an Israeli soldier who had been killed. Isaac felt sorry for her. He tried to love her, I guess. He wrote his parents, and they came to visit him in Israel. They told him they were happy and proud.

"Jimmy heard them tell this story to his parents. They were so stupid. All of them thought they were geniuses.

"They told Annie that Isaac had gotten married, that now she had to get over him. I saw Annie almost every day at school. She began going over to the Hillel office to speak with the rabbi there. She didn't tell me about what they discussed, but she began asking me questions, reading books. Maybe, I thought, she was just confused.

"Her parents tried to arrange for her to meet someone they liked. She did go one with one man, but she told her brother when she came home she was physically sick.

"It's been several years now, grandpa. They haven't been in touch. As far as I know they are both miserable."

"And this Jimmy?"

"Yes, Jimmy. Grandpa, that's why I'm here. Jimmy is more grown up now. He understands more. He's still a teenager, but he's a smart one. Grandpa, do you understand? He was crying when he called me to tell the story. He had to get it out. He said he wants to tell his sister. He said this is the last big chance because Isaac is coming back to the United States. He even knew the flight. But his choice is to betray his parents or his sister. That's no choice at all. He didn't know what to do. And he asked me. And now I ask you, grandpa, what should I tell him?"

"You want me to relieve you of making this decision?"

"No, grandpa. I want your advice. I know I have to make it myself. I know it's easy to tell him to speak with Annie. But then I bear the responsibility if his own relationship with his parents deteriorates."

"Good. You see this is not as easy as it looks. Is this Jimmy old enough to make his own decisions?"

"I think he is. But I can't just say that to him. I have to help."

"I understand. I wanted some assessment of his abilities."

"He's old enough."

"Then, Lily, I do have an observation. Sometimes when we ask advice, we know what we want to do but need to have that verified by someone we trust. Jimmy could have asked a family member, say an aunt or an uncle, for advice."

"But they would have told him not to tell Annie supposedly for her own good."

"Yes, naturally, they would. And Jimmy knew that consciously or at some deeper level. Similarly, Lily, he knew if he asked you that your loyalty was to his sister not his parents."

"You mean he wants me to tell him to speak with Annie?"

"Yes, I believe he does. He needs your help to gather up his courage, but that's what he wants to do."

"Not bad, grandpa."

"You see, the cursed sun hasn't fried my brain."

"Thank goodness for that. Stay here, grandpa, I'm going inside and call Jimmy."

When I returned, my grandfather was at our fence talking to a neighbor. He said good-bye and came back to sit down.

"Jimmy sounded very relieved," I said. "He's going to call his sister tonight."

"Very good. I hope it all works out."

"Are you rooting for love here grandpa? If love wins, then so does an intermarriage."

"I root for people. That's all I can do in life."

I thought my grandfather had evaded my question, but I let it go.

"Can I ask you now about searching for my other grandfather?"

"Sure."

"Okay. So, as you know, his name was Leopold Siegel. But we don't know where he was born, when he came here, when he died, or where he is buried. It's like he was born from the air. Papa doesn't remember much about him. When I was growing up, papa didn't speak so much of his parents. His mother even died when he was young, but he remembers her because he was twenty when she passed on. What can I do to find Leopold Siegel?"

My grandfather scratched his face. "He died in New York?"

"Yes. I know that. My father was living then on the Lower East Side, I think on East Houston."

"If he died in New York, they kept a record of it."

"I don't know where to look. I just have his name."

"Where is your father's mama buried?"

"At Mt. Zion." It was a big cemetery.

"And you've been there?"

"Yes, and he's not buried next to her."

"Very unusual, but it happened. A woman says she saw enough of him in life she doesn't want to spend eternity by his side.

"What does your father remember about the day of his papa's funeral?"

"Not much. He remembers that it was cloudy. He went home and cried and listened all night to the radio. He remembers that very well."

"What did he hear on the radio?"

I looked at my grandfather. "I don't know."

"Go inside and ask him."

My father knew immediately, and I came back out. "My father was seven, so it was sometime in 1934. He listened to what he could all night. He does remember best a Burns and Allen show. It was about coming to America."

"Did you ever hear of radio logs?"

"No, grandpa."

"There are fans, like movie or tv fans. Radio fans kept track of different shows. I know a dealer. Let's see if he's got what we need."

We walked inside, and my father placed a call. He listened and jotted down some information on a piece of paper.

"We're lucky. The notes the dealer had did not include much information from 1934. But there was a Burns and Allen program titled 'Leaving For America' that aired on September 26, 1934. It was a Wednesday."

"But what do I do with that, grandpa?"

"You figure your grandfather Leopold died on Tuesday, September 25th. You call the cemetery again and ask if they have a Siegel who died that day buried there. And you ask what section of the cemetery he's buried in if he's there, what society was he part of if any."

First I was confused, and then I was amazed. When I finished I turned to my grandfather.

"He's buried there under his nickname, Lipa, and Siegel isn't spelled the way my father spells the name. And he was buried under…" I showed my grandfather the society.

"People from the same town in Europe came here and established societies. For a small price the poor Jews could purchase a burial plot." My grandfather pointed. "He came from Rava Ruska. So now you research that."

I'll always remember that day, because it was one on which my grandfather's brain shone brightly. It was one on which we worked together to solve problems.

I went on to create an incredible family tree, and I found my place on it. I saw where I was in the family the branches that went back and sidewards, and I envisioned the branches that would extend further. The sight of the tree balanced an isolation I often felt, but it added to a burden, that I had to earn my place on that tree. Family gave me a home and a responsibility. I made photocopies of the tree and kept one with me. When I needed to do so, I looked at it. When I felt alone, when I felt defeated, when I felt angry at one member of the family or another or at myself or at history or at people or at God, I looked and looked at that tree. It was part of me.

And family was part of Jimmy. He told Annie the story. They drove out to the airport together to meet Isaac's plane.

When Isaac got off, she saw in the distance how his shoulders sagged, how sad he looked. Jimmy told her to wait, that he would speak to Isaac. Jimmy ran ahead. Isaac looked up. Slowly, calmly Jimmy told him the story. Isaac almost fainted. Annie could see him reach out for Jimmy to hold him up.

When Jimmy finished telling the story, Annie ran up to Isaac. They hugged. The three of them went to get some coffee. Slowly the whole story came out. They each told their side and Jimmy filled in the rest. Isaac said he had ended his marriage soon after it began. He was horrified as he heard the details of what his parents and her parents had done.

And, then, Annie asked Jimmy if he would mind waiting outside the restaurant, that she had some important words to say to Isaac. Jimmy was glad, glad his sister had forgiven him, glad they were so happy to see each other.

When Jimmy left, Annie cried again. She said that three weeks after Isaac left she had wondered why she loved him so much, why his values meant so much to her. And she had concluded that he was Jewish in a way his father would never be, that he understood the Jewish moral outlook meant more than the rituals his father practiced. She told him she realized that in loving him she had learned about and wanted to explore Judaism. She told him she had gone to see a Hillel rabbi and asked about becoming Jewish. He had told her it was a Jewish tradition to discourage would-be converts to make sure they were sincere, that there was much to learn and study if she wished to continue.

Isaac sat and listened and told her she didn't need to become Jewish for him. She said she wanted to become Jewish for herself, that she had gone through with the conversion believing that she might never see Isaac again. She said she had taken the Hebrew name of Ruth.

She told me this story as we walked on campus.

When she finished the story, I hugged her.

And it was at that moment that she invited me to her wedding. She said, after all, I was in spirit already part of the family.

CHAPTER SEVENTEEN:
GRANDPA'S STORY

Sometimes when I'm walking and not even thinking about him, some story about my grandfather will enter my mind. I'll smile, get a mental image of him, and remember. Maybe I'm just wandering down a street, and I look into a window and see an older man. For a minute, he's my grandfather. He's inside the store waiting for me. He'll wonder where I've been, how I've been doing. He'll ask about my writing. And then I look carefully, and it's not my grandfather at all, just some stranger. And I should know better, but I'm disappointed because grandpa isn't there with me. When that happened I used to call him, and we'd laugh about it. He'd tell me he was really there, that he'd discovered the trick of being in two places at once.

There must be a thousand stories about my grandfather, because he was always there in my youth and at every stage for any reason I sought him out. He always had a tale to tell, a proverb to offer, gathered from somewhere in the Jewish past. A half-truth is a whole lie he'd tell me. Once I told him how proud I was of myself for telling the truth. He said what I had done was right but I should remember that I could only call myself honest if I first had a chance to steal. I once asked him if he was good on account of God. He shrugged and said, "I tell people that if you won't be good because of God, be good for selfish reasons. Being moral leads to a happy and productive life." He was like a proverb jukebox. I'd press a button, and out would come some bit of wisdom, some guideline for me to remember.

There were sad moments for him, of course, especially after my grandmother died. And he couldn't always take the advice he offered. One of his favorite stories, taken from Jewish literature, was about Solomon, the wisest person who ever lived. Solomon, my grandfather said, got a beautiful new ring, and he wanted to carve a saying on it, but not just any saying. No, he wanted the wisest words he could find. He sought advice, he asked all, and one day he decided on the words he carved on that ring. The words were "This, too, shall pass." Whenever he was sad, Solomon could look down at the ring and read the words and be reassured that the world would right itself again. But, my grandfather reminded me, when all was going well, when the rhythms of the cosmos were all in tune, he would look down at the ring and read it again. Then he would realize that this happiness, this joy, would not last long either. I reminded my grandfather of that saying after my grandmother died, but he had trouble believing it any longer.

My grandfather told me he had lived too long, that he had outlived his energy and the passions that ignited his life. For the last year, he has told me he was tired of London, a reference, he said, to Samuel Johnson who believed that a person tired of London was tired of life.

I feel guilty because I didn't try to cheer my grandfather up enough. I was leading my own life, and my grandfather told me he wanted me to do that. He told me to cherish my freedom and my youth.

My grandfather taught me to wrap myself in words, to write honestly. But he also taught me that words have borders, and that we need to cross the borders into the real world to make it better.

In the final years of my graduate work, my grandfather got more and more interested in Jews trapped in the Soviet Union. He did this in his struggle against age, against his own feelings of having no purpose. He battled with himself. And what a battle. He wrote letters for the Jews. He went into visit his Congressman. The Congressman was overwhelmed by this older man armed with knowledge and charm. My grandfather went to seders, to seniors groups. He talked about Soviet Jews wherever he could.

He kept track as Jewish families went to Israel. And, miracle of miracles, he heard about Mendel, the boy he had told me about who had been taken by the Russian army. Mendel's great-grandchildren had been allowed to move to Israel, just as Mendel's children had dreamed about. My grandfather called Mendel's great-grandchildren. They exchanged stories. My grandfather didn't tell anyone, but he sent them money and gifts.

Each year there was a protest on behalf of the Jews who couldn't leave or were imprisoned. The protest took place at the Soviet compound in Glen Cove. Since we lived in Nassau County, he felt that whatever his age he had to go.

He invited me along, and I happily agreed to join him.

First, we went to a delicatessen for dinner. It was summertime, and we were waiting for darkness so that the candlelight vigil that we were to be part of would include lights that shone brightly.

My grandfather was eighty-two, but that didn't stop him from ordering a big corn beef sandwich with some matzoh ball soup. We ate quietly for a few minutes, and then he said, "I wonder how many more corned beef sandwiches I will have."

I looked at him. "Did you ever think you'd live this long, grandpa?"

He smiled. "Never. Of course, now that I've gotten this far, I wouldn't mind seeing what happens over the next few years. And on a good morning when I look in the mirror I don't see this old face. I see a nineteen year old boy staring back at me, eager to explore life. On a bad morning I won't say what I see."

He sipped some water. "It's an adventure getting old, Lily. It's not for the weak."

He hesitated.

"What's the matter, grandpa?"

"I was going to say some words that I shouldn't."

"Grandpa, have we ever held back from each other?"

"No, we haven't." Again he paused. "I was going to say that meaning has a way of slipping away, that the whole point of it all made more sense to me thirty years ago than it does now. I don't think that's so good to say to someone young."

"If you don't think life has any meaning anymore, Grandpa, why are we going to this vigil tonight?"

"In my confusion I keep acting like I always did. I just have doubts now. I just wonder if it all isn't simply nonsense. But I keep going the way I did because I don't know how else to act."

"Maybe you feel like that because it's a way your mind is preparing for death, making it easier to accept death by robbing what you're leaving behind of the meaning it once had."

He looked up at me. "I'm proud of you, Lily."

No words ever meant more to me.

"Thanks, grandpa." Now I was the one who hesitated.

"What is it?"

"I was just curious, grandpa. You haven't ever talked to me about it. Do you believe in life after death?"

He held up his hands. "Who knows? I have enough trouble thinking about life. I don't think there is, but I'm prepared to be surprised. I expect everyone at my funeral will say, 'Oh, Benjamin is at peace now, happily reunited with his wife, annoying God with endless questions.' And maybe it will happen. And sometimes I think there has to be a Heaven because how else could God provide justice? It certainly isn't here on Earth.

"Whatever happens, I don't want people to sob for me or feel sorry for me. I don't want to be mourned. Don't cry too much for me when the time comes, Lily."

"What should I do, grandpa?"

"Remember me in your own way. That's all."

"You can be sure I'll do that, grandpa."

And after dinner, I drove my grandfather to the vigil.

There was a fair-sized crowd. I was bothered because I saw some young men across the way. They were yelling at those by the compound, screaming out at them, taunting them. I stared at the men. They were fueled by hatred and confusion. None of it made sense to me.

They were screaming at us as we walked by.

"Hey old man," one man screamed at my grandfather. "They should lock you up."

My grandfather stopped.

The young man who had screamed began to walk forward toward us.

"Come on, grandpa, let's go. Forget him."

My grandfather didn't respond.

The man kept walking toward us. Two of his friends, one on either side, went with him.

He stopped when he was about ten feet from us.

"They should lock you all up," he said.

"Then who would you have to yell at?"

The man took three steps forward.

"What did you say?"

"I said, you'll have to keep yelling at everyone. The decent people are all on the same side. There's too many of us now. You won't be able to yell at all of us."

"Then I'll just yell at you. That's enough, old man."

The man looked around, found a rock, and picked it up. "Here, have some exercise."

He threw the rock, and my grandfather stepped off to one side.

"You're pretty fast, old man. But not fast enough. There are a lot of us with a lot of rocks."

Just then a police officer walked up and said, "Is there any trouble?"

"That man threw a rock at my grandfather." I pointed.

The man smiled. "I was showing it to a friend, and it slipped."

"Is anyone hurt?" the policeman asked.

"Nah," the man said, "Not me and not that old man. Not yet."

"That's a threat," I said.

The policeman went over to talk to the young men, and they walked away.

My grandfather shook his head. "I wish I was fifty years younger."

"It's good that you're not grandpa. I don't want you hurt."

"You have to stand up for yourself, Lily. They should free a lunatic and lock him up."

I remained silent. We walked over to stand among those at the vigil. My grandfather went to the organizer, a woman he knew well. We stood silently for an hour. The crowd across from us continued to yell.

It was about ten o'clock when the police officer came up to us. He walked over to the woman in charge. "There's a credible bomb threat that was just called in," he said, his voice even and almost in a whisper. "Those young men over there are serious. This is not a good night to be out here. I think you ought to break it up and go home. No one thought they'd be trouble and there aren't any other police officers here to stop whatever might happen. I've called for help, but it may take a while."

My grandfather turned to the woman. "What are you going to do?"

She shook her head. "I'm going to stay. How would it look if we ran while there are so many prisoners in the Soviet Union?"

My grandfather nodded, and he turned to me.

"Lily, I'm going to stay, too, but you are young. Go away and come back in an hour for me."

"Is that what you're trying to teach me, grandpa? To run when there's trouble? Didn't you just tell me when that man threw a rock at you that we have to stand up to those who would hurt us?"

"I'm your grandfather, and I'm trying to keep you safe."

"Safety is for a different world, grandpa, not this one."

"Oy. If the bomb doesn't kill me, your mother will."

"I'm staying, grandpa. It's my decision to make, and I'm making it."

He nodded. It was dark, but I thought I saw a smile.

We stood there at our candlelight vigil. There was no bomb, only continuing taunts from the men across the way. Finally, it was time to leave.

The whole group of us started to go. The men followed us, yelling the whole way. And then they began to throw rocks. The stones were flying through the air. I could almost hear them. One hit a man next to me.

The moonlight was bright, and I could just about see the men's faces in the distance. I saw the rocks flying, but didn't know what to do. All of a sudden, with my grandfather beside me, I saw a rock coming at him. He was half-turned and couldn't see it coming. I wasn't strong enough to push him out of the way, and there wasn't time for him to react if I yelled.

I stepped in front of him with my hands up, but somehow the rock went through my open arms and hit the side of my head.

I remember the pain, and I remember falling, but after that I only know what happened because people told me. I collapsed. There was blood flowing from me at an ever-quickening pace. The people around me screamed. A police car showed up and drove me and my grandfather to the hospital. The men throwing the rocks had disappeared. They must have run away when they saw the police.

I woke up in the emergency room, a nurse leaning over me.

"You'll be fine," she assured me. "It's a cut. I wouldn't enter any beauty contests this week if I were you, but there's no real damage."

"How's my grandfather?"

"He's very upset. He's in the waiting room. He keeps asking about you. I think he likes you a little."

I just lay there for what seemed like several more hours. The nurse came back a few times. A doctor came by once. Then the nurse returned, smiling. "Good news. The doctor said you don't even have to stay overnight. They did an x-ray, they did a bunch of tests, and all of it was very good. You're young, and I'm sure that helped. The doctor said you can go whenever you feel like it. My advice is to rest. You may feel a bit dizzy just from lying down. "

"I'd like to try to stand up. Can you help me?"

"Of course." I put my legs over the edge of the bed, and began to stand, leaning on the nurse's shoulder. My head was dizzy, and my knees felt weak. I waited a few minutes until I was sure I could walk on my own.

"I'll need a ride home."

"Your parents are waiting with your grandfather. I think they already went to get your car."

"Good."

I walked slowly, but I was proud of myself. I had stood my ground. I had protected my grandfather. My head was spinning, and I almost fell a few times, but I walked slowly.

And then I saw them. They were all seated, chatting quietly. I smiled and began to walk to them.

As I approached, I said, "I'm fine. Let's just get out of here. I really need a piece of chocolate cake."

My father smiled. My mother looked anxious but relieved.

My grandfather fell forward out of his chair onto the floor. My mother screamed. I closed my eyes, opened them quickly, and bent over.

His face looked calm, completely at peace. I reached down to touch him.

A nurse came running toward us. She bent down next to my grandfather.

He died fifteen minutes later. The doctor told us it was from a massive stroke. I had saved him, and then I had killed him.

Somehow, on the ride home, I kept thinking of Dennis Bello, the boy from my youth I thought I had hit with a rock. I knew what my grandfather would have said, that this was my atonement from that episode because I had been hit by a rock myself, and let that happen voluntarily to protect a loved one. I knew my grandfather would have been proud of me. I knew the fault lay with the men who had hurled those rocks, and with the hatred that led them to attack us. The problem was, on that miserable ride back home, that even knowing all that I still couldn't forgive myself.

I spoke at the funeral. I told them the story of the vigil. As I got to my grandfather's collapse, my hands were shaking, and my head felt very dizzy. I began to cry. I was upset with myself. My mother had asked me if I was capable of delivering the eulogy, and I had said I was. Standing there, I wasn't sure if I could finish.

I looked over the crowd. I was surprised to see Mr. Goldberg sitting out there. He must have struggled to come to a funeral, but this one was for his friend.

Everyone was patient, staring at me silently, waiting for me to continue with my speech. I stared at my parents, at my older brother. I stared at family members, all the people from the neighborhood, all of my grandfather's friends. They were kind, knowing the pain I was in, knowing that I blamed myself. I gripped the lectern, felt a toughened part of me rising knowing my grandfather would have wanted me to continue. It took about twenty seconds for the wave of sorrow to lessen enough for me to continue. My head was spinning, but I continued on with my speech.

When my grandfather died, I told them, I saw a lifetime of wisdom in his face. I told them that my grandfather had once written me that a person can study for seventy years and still die a fool. I continued talking.

My grandfather didn't die a fool, I told them. He died as a sacred man. He said he didn't know the destination of his soul. I said that I know that if there's a God up there, God will be lucky to meet my grandfather. They will have a lot to talk about.

I thanked them all for coming, for listening to me.

And then, as I stepped down to wait for the next speaker, I reached the bottom step and fainted.

People rushed toward me. I saw my mother's face above me crying.

I opened my eyes. Someone gave me a cup of water. Deeply embarrassed, I got up and let my parents guide me back to sit down. I was fine for the rest of the funeral.

The police never caught the person who threw the rock at my grandfather.

Eleven days after the burial, I sat down to write a story about my grandfather and me, about the time I was a little girl. Only it was fiction, so I changed it. I made me a male and my grandfather into my grandmother. That provided enough emotional distance. Otherwise I'm not sure I could have written much.

The words flowed. I remembered all that he had said. And then, in the middle of the story, I stopped. I shivered. Was I being fair, writing about my grandfather? Or was I using his for my own purposes? I wish my grandfather were around to help me solve that. I tried to think in the way he would.

I walked around the block. When I got home I took down some books and began reading. I walked out into the night to look at the stars.

I returned to my typewriter and my memories. And I felt a power. I should have had my Bat Mitzvah that night, for it was then that I felt like an adult, that my grandfather had been working all those years to prepare me for this day, that the story would forever connect me to his memory. I went back to writing. I finished and re-wrote the story. Then I put it away and went back to it the next day. I re-wrote it again. I carried the story around in my mind and jotted down ideas when I had them, which always seemed to occur at odd moments even moments when my mind was thinking about another subject.

I ended up re-writing the story eight times. I knew the magazine where I wanted to send it, so I wrote a cover letter and mailed off my memory and my future.

The story came back a week later. As I stood at the mailbox, I was profoundly disappointed and incredibly sad. It was a slow walk back to the kitchen table where I opened the envelope that I had addressed and stamped.

I looked inside. The story was there but so was a note from the editor. There were some suggestions to improve the story.

I ran to my room and re-wrote the story feverishly. The editor's ideas prompted some thoughts of my own. I considered making my grandfather a co-author. He would have waved his hand at me and given me one of his sayings. I smiled. I paced thinking of what words my grandfather had taught me. It was then that I felt the irony. In life, my grandfather was often not around, especially in the previous few years. But in death, there he was, always available to me through the vividness of the memories. It was as though his death had sealed his memory for me in a way that made it pulsate with its presence.

I re-wrote the story three times more, understanding a lot from what the editor had suggested. Finally, satisfied that I written as well as I could, I returned the story.

A few days later the editor accepted my story, the first one that I ever got published.

I stared at that letter, and it made me believe that my grandfather would never truly die, that this was his story.

CHAPTER EIGHTEEN:
THE EIGHTEENTH DREAM

A month and a day after the funeral, I got a call. It was Mr. Goldberg. He said he wanted to meet me, that he was obligated to meet me. We arranged to meet in front of the New York Public Library the next day at noon.

I was already waiting, sitting on the steps, when I saw him trudging along. He saw me standing up and waving at him. He waved back.

We met, and he smiled at me.

"It's nice to see you again, Lily."

"You, too, Mr. Goldberg."

"Please, you're old enough now. Call me just Goldberg, like my friends do."

"That's not so easy."

"It gets easier." He paused. "Your grandfather was the nicest man I ever knew. Not so good at cards, but good at nice."

"Thank you."

He nodded. Clearly, he had words he wanted to say but was having trouble saying them. "You knew he was a journalist. I bet you didn't know he published a little book about his ideas."

I was stunned. "No," I said. "No one, including him, ever told me that."

"I know. He was a little shy. He thought he was just a journalist, good enough for a newspaper that would be gone in a day, not so good for more enduring literature."

Goldberg reached into his packet and pulled out a slim volume. It was called *The Land of Eighteen Dreams* and, there was my grandfather's name, Benjamin Kagan.

"It's a book of his thoughts, sort of an intellectual memoir," Goldberg said. "He told me he wrote poems in his youth and stories, but I never saw them. I imagine they are long gone. I also have collected some of his articles." Again he reached in and brought out a small folder. "I'm sorry. I don't have so many, but the ones I have are for you."

"You're giving me these?"

Goldberg shrugged. "Who else should have them?"

"That's very kind of you. Do you want to have some lunch?"

"Thank you. A small lunch would be good. Afterwards, I have a meeting. Oy, it's a full-time job being Jewish.

"I just wanted to give you this and see your face when I did."

"I've often thought about what you told me, Mr....I mean Goldberg. I'm sorry I can't do it. Please, as a favor, Mr. Goldberg."

He gave a short nod. "So what did you think so much about?"

"About being good, and God, and finding all my missions. I wrote it all down after I came home. And last year I read the book you gave me by Abraham Joshua Heschel. Now I understand it. Now I think about what I should do in life."

"So your conscience has been busy. This is a good sign. I hope for your sake it does not pester you quite so much at odd moments in the night."

I smiled. "So far, my conscience has gone to sleep when I do."

"A well-trained conscience. The best kind."

We walked over to a nearby restaurant, sat down, and ordered.

"Your grandfather called me two days ago, Lily. We spoke for a long while. Neither of us knew it would be the finishing conversation, but as I look back it was fitting. Your grandfather talked a lot about you, Lily. He was proud, of course, but that's not what he discussed."

I couldn't respond, so I just looked at Mr. Goldberg.

"Your grandfather did much good in his life, for many people that he met, for the Jewish people. But he has been worried for the past ten or even more years. He was worried that he was getting so old that he couldn't perform his missions in life.

"It would have been no greater honor for him to defend Soviet Jews as his last act. He was spared the fate he dreaded, living out a life without being able to affect the world.

"But, Lily, he came to realize that his final mission was not helping the Soviet Jews. He came to realize that you were his final mission."

"Me?"

"Yes. He didn't think of you as a carbon copy of him. He wouldn't want that. He wanted you to find your own way. He said he once told you about the poem he learned as a child, about eighteen dreams."

I nodded.

"Seeing you grow up to be a good person was his eighteenth dream, Lily. And he saw it. How many of us get to see our eighteenth dream come true? Not so many."

"But if not for me, he would have lived."

"If not for you he would have been hit in the head and died. Instead, at the very end, he saw his granddaughter was a hero. You could not have given him a greater gift."

Mr. Goldberg looked down. "There are some people who say the body has a soul. I studied with some Kabbalists in Israel in my youth, and they taught me that it is the soul that has a body. That's why we have to take care of our bodies, to protect our souls that have much to do in life. Your grandfather's soul used the body it was given to do good, and he wanted to see the soul you were given do good as well. Your grandfather taught me that if you know how to do right, you will know all there is to know and all you need to know. Truth isn't beauty. Truth is goodness."

We ate for a while.

"Tell me, Lily, you're so young. What job do you have?"

"I will finish graduate school soon, Mr. Goldberg. I teach some undergraduates now. I thought I would spend my life as a sociology professor, but last year I changed my mind. I've been doing a lot of reading of Jewish texts and history and novels. I'm going to become a Jewish journalist."

"Oy. And what will you do for a living?"

"That's funny, Mr. Goldberg. I'll keep writing. I'll do what I have to do. I hope to get married, too. I think that's part of my mission."

He nodded. "Very nice. And where will you do this Jewish journalism?"

"I have an interview next week with Irving Weinglass. You know him?"

"Who doesn't know the meshuggenah Irving Weinglass? God forgot to put a pause button on his mouth."

"There's a job at the paper."

Mr. Goldberg nodded. "He's not such a nice man, Irving Weinglass."

"I've heard that."

"Whatever you heard isn't so bad as the real him."

"I want to try."

Mr. Goldberg had finished his lunch, waited until I finished mine, and then he called for the check.

"I'll pay for my meal, Mr. Goldberg."

"And your grandfather would strike me down from Heaven if I let you pay. Please. Let me protect myself."

We parted. I walked into the New York Public Library, sat down, and opened my grandfather's book.

It wasn't what I expected. There were fragments, almost journal entries. Brief thoughts, and then longer ones. I looked at the headline of one of them: THE MONSTER COMEDIAN.I began reading.

I wasn't so young when television began, so I could follow the growth of comedians on television, the quiet ones like Jack Benny or George Burns, or the maniacal ones like Jerry Lewis, or the loud ones like Sid Caesar and Milton Berle. But I could not understand the appeal of Dizzy Gardner, born Goldstein. He reminded me of the man who wanted to marry my sister. Dizzy was on every week, squirting bottles and throwing pies like Soupy Sales, talking in funny accents like Caesar, intruding on everyone's act like Berle.

One day, I was given the assignment to write a profile of Dizzy Gardner. I went backstage. He wasn't wearing his pants. This was quite common. Comedians and other performers didn't want to wrinkle the pants by wearing them before the show. Dizzy had two women in the room, and a large number of bottles of wine.

"Ah, the reporter." He signaled me to come sit near him. He sent the women outside.

"I see you looking at those women in a disapproving way. Let me tell you, a sin is only difficult the first time. Then you get used to it. Then you like it. Your name is Benjamin?"

"Yes."

"So, Benjamin, tell me why do you do this? I shouldn't be talking to you. I should only do television interviews. No one reads anymore. They spend their times looking and listening. They use their eyes and ears more than their brains. That's good for me, not so good for you."

"Can I quote you?"

He laughed loudly. "Quote all you want. My publicist will call you a liar. It will be good publicity."

His eyes narrowed. "You're a loser, Benjamin. You write for a nothing publication about a great man like me. Why do you waste your life like this? You lead this narrow life. Why do I need the Jews? I have my sponsors and my audience. They're much better than the Jews. They give me money. They laugh when I tell jokes. Who laughs at you, Benjamin? Behind your back they mock you, am I right? You lead a little Jewish life. Let the adults lead a real life. Ah, I pity you. You look around, and you'll wish you were me. I have it all. What do you have?"

I was shocked. He didn't want me to write a profile. He wanted to attack me.

"Mr. Gardner."

"Mr. Gardner? I thought you were ready to call me Goldstein. That's why you're here isn't it? To tell the Jews how lucky they are to have me as one of theirs. You tell your readers I'm a comedian, I'm not a Jewish comedian. I'm funny. I'm not Jewish funny. I'm a person, not a Jewish person."

I stood up and started to walk out, turned back, and said. "I don't know if I'm talking to the former Mr. Goldstein or the current Mr. Gardner. Either one is a monster. I understand why you mock me and mock the Jews. If you didn't you'd have to see your true self, beneath your expensive clothes and the make-up that you think hides you. I'm not going to write about you. Let the television stations do it. I'm going to write about decent human beings."

Gardner picked up a bottle of wine and threw it at me. I stepped out of the way.

"You think you're throwing this at me. You're throwing this at the man you used to be and can never be again."

Then I went outside. My editor wasn't too happy with me. The paper had already promised readers a profile of Dizzy

Gardner. I got stuck writing articles on subjects I didn't like for a while.

I always think of Dizzy Gardner as the man an American Jew can become.

The story ended there. I began reading some more. Eventually, I returned to my apartment, clutching my grandfather's words tightly.

Over the following week I read and re-read the words my grandfather had written. I followed his tales, the characters he had met, the lines he wrote. I wish my eighteenth dream could have been to bring him back.

He did write about the eighteenth dream:

The Land of Eighteen Dreams isn't just in America. It's anywhere people are free to hurt others but help instead, anywhere control beats temptation to the mouth, anywhere kindness is as reflexive as breathing. This is the land we must find and explore, the land where the unblinking confrontation of reality doesn't lead to bitterness or cynicism. Nor is it a land in which we smile and pretend humans will be good if only given a chance. No, in the Land of Eighteen Dreams, we aren't lambs. We're soldiers when we have to be and artists when we can be. Sometimes we are in grief. Sometimes we are in despair. Sometimes we don't even believe in our own dreams. And yet we go on, for the Land of Eighteen Dreams, fragile and cracked though it may be, always stretches infinitely before us.

I typed out that passage and pasted it over my typewriter.

Finally, it was time for my job interview. I dressed carefully, reviewed what I wanted to say, and took a subway to meet Irving Weinglass.

His office was packed beyond belief. Every corner was stacked with newspapers. Books were placed every which way in his bookcases. Weinglass himself was very thin. He always seemed to be moving some part of himself.

I walked in. He kept writing, and then peered over his glasses. I looked at his red face, his thinning, curly brown hair. He looked back at me for a few seconds, and then he said, "Why should I give you a job?"

"Because I'll make you look like a great editor."

"I have no need for you to make me look like anyone. I am a great editor. Go away. You have no experience. My dog knows more about Jewish life than you do."

"I'm not leaving, Mr. Weinglass. I belong here. Perhaps your dog and I can co-write some articles."

"Hmm. Do you know that to write about Jewish life you should know about ten or so languages? Do you know them?"

"I only have to write in one language, Mr. Weinglass. And I can do that."

"You're too young. You'll quit to get married and have some little darlings."

"Men don't quit when they get married or have children. Doing both helps them understand Jewish life and the world better."

"So you think you have answers, huh? Well, do you have an answer to the fact that to do this job you should have spent a lifetime on the sea of Talmud? That you need to know 5,000 years of history and all that's going on today?"

"I know what I don't know, Mr. Weinglass. Isn't that the beginning of wisdom?"

"Twenty people want this job. Everybody goes to college now and still they don't read books. They don't write. I don't know why you want this job. I'm very mean."

"So my grandfather told me."

"A smart man. Who is this genius?"

"He died recently. His name was Benjamin Kagan."

He stopped writing at his desk and looked up at me.

"You are Benny Kagan's granddaughter?"

"I'm his daughter Devorah's child."

Weinglass sat back in his chair and pursed his lips. "I read about his death. I'm sorry."

"Thank you."

He reached into his desk, pulled out a yellowed piece of paper, and handed it to me. "Go off into the corner into the next office and write me an obituary. I've written down some facts about the person's life."

I nodded, took the sheet, found my seat and began writing.

When I finished, I walked back to the office and gave it to him.

He read it over slowly. Then he read it again.

"You're no Benny Kagan, I can tell you that. He knew how to write an obituary." He paused. "Still, it isn't bad. You know the pay?"

"Yes."

He nodded. "You'll have to unlearn a lot that you got with your fancy degrees."

"I'm ready."

"So your grandfather told you I was mean."

"He wasn't the only one."

"It's nice to have a reputation. So why do you want to learn from such a mean man?"

"My grandfather told me no one could teach me more about being a Jewish journalist."

"I always knew Benny Kagan was a wise man. I want you to understand, I wouldn't care if you were King David's granddaughter, if you couldn't write I wouldn't want you. I don't do favors for people I know."

"My grandfather wouldn't have wanted you to and neither do I."

"Okay, as long as we understand that. You're a decent writer for your age. I may be able to teach you a bit. It won't be easy."

"I wouldn't want it to be."

"My brother is a rabbi. He likes to tell people that the gates of prayer are never locked. I like to tell people that the gates of this office are never locked. You'll have very long hours."

"When can I begin?"

"This minute. Go to that hideous old man out there and tell him I want you to cover the Jewish film festival. And you better do a good job."

"Thank you Mr. Weinglass."

"We'll see if you're thanking me in two weeks."

And so my writing career began.

And that led to all the rest.

Now, after it all, I have finally discovered my eighteenth dream.

This book about my grandfather and me is my eighteenth dream, these memories of the moments when I walked through the fog and the darkness and came to a place where I learned to live, these words that seek to preserve the relationship that gave me life.

Now I live in the Land of Eighteen Dreams.

AUTHOR'S NOTE

This book is a work of fiction. The characters and incidents are imagined. Any actual historical figures and events are used fictitiously. In the first chapter, for example, I have extended the rules for conscription beyond the time they existed in Russian history.

ABOUT THE AUTHOR

Lawrence J. Epstein is a former professor of English at Suffolk Community College on Long Island where he taught courses in writing and journalism as well as courses on Jewish Thought and the Holocaust. He is the author of such Jewish-related books as *At the Edge of a Dream: The Story of Jewish Immigrants on New York's Lower East Side*, 1880-1920 (Jossey-Bass/Lower East Side Tenement Museum, 2007), *The Haunted Smile: The Story of Jewish Comedians in America* (PublicAffairs, 2001), *A Treasury of Jewish Inspirational Stories* (Jason Aronson, 1993), *A Treasury of Jewish Anecdotes* (Jason Aronson, 1989), and *Zion's Call: Christian Contributions to the Origins and Development of Israel* (University Press of America, 1984). He has written a variety of other books as well as over a hundred articles on Jewish subjects for such places as *The Jerusalem Post*.

CPSIA information can be obtained at www.ICGtesting.com
Printed in the USA
BVOW040108310112

281670BV00001B/3/P